APRIL SHOWERS BRING DEAD FLOWERS

KRISTA LOCKHEART

NEXT CHAPTER PUBLISHING

To my creative team for brainstorming with me this fascinating and funny cozy mystery.

WANT TO RECEIVE UPDATES FROM KRISTA ABOUT HER NEW BOOKS?

If you'd like to receive notifications when I send out free previews of my next books, you can sign up for my newsletter here:

https://kristalockheartauthor.com

ONE

If it wasn't for the alarm on her cell phone sounding like an air raid strike, Heather Moore might not have woken up that morning to head to the Cambridge Flower Market. She bolted up in her bed immediately, not entirely sure if she was dreaming or wide awake. Then, as soon as she saw the pile of boxes across the other side of her bedroom, she calmed down, remembering that was exactly how she left it several hours ago when she went to bed.

She looked down at her cell phone—3:00 a.m., about the right time to fight the crowd for the special flower she needed. It would take her an hour to get there, so she had just enough time to make breakfast for both her and Ant, her rambunctious chihuahua who still lay sleeping next to her. Heather nudged him a bit, and he growled back at her. He clearly didn't understand how important today was to her, so she nudged him again.

"Come on, sleepyhead! It's time to get going," Heather said softly. "The crazy crowds at the flower market wait for no one." Ant snorted at her and cuddled up closer, attempting to go right back to sleep. "Okay, maybe we can wait five more minutes. But we can't put it off for much longer than that." As he slept peacefully in her arms, she stroked his silky fur to calm her nerves until he eventually gave in to her prodding and bounded off the bed and downstairs for his morning walk.

After a few minutes, they returned, and Heather took containers out of the refrigerator to prepare a quick gourmet omelet she'd been craving for the past week. Avocados. Fresh tomatoes. Homegrown herbs. Fresh organic eggs from the farmer's market. Artesian cheeses. *Oh, my!* Heather practically salivated for that first bite as the egg and herb mixture bubbled in the cast-iron skillet she'd inherited from her grandmother. Like the house she had just moved into, this skillet was a family heirloom passed down from generation to generation.

Tossing the cheese, vegetables, and avocado slices into the pan, Heather turned around to see Ant sniffing around for his breakfast. Like he normally did every morning, he started talking nonstop in a language only Heather understood. This morning, though, he seemed extra put out that she hadn't fed him yet.

"I know, I know! I'm a very bad Mommy." She took out a container of pre-boiled eggs she'd prepared the night before and mashed it up for his breakfast. Tossing some fresh spinach into the bowl, she looked down to see Ant licking his chops and wagging his tail. "Can you ever forgive me?" Heather placed the bowl on the kitchen table, and Ant jumped up into his booster chair to eat his breakfast.

When she finally sat down to eat her own breakfast, she let out a slight sigh of happiness because it was everything she expected it to be and more. It didn't take either of them long to finish eating, so Heather let Ant out in the backyard for a few minutes while she showered and got ready to leave. When she returned to the kitchen, she found Ant asleep in front of the back door.

STILL DARK OUTSIDE BECAUSE OF THE EARLY HOUR, HEATHER tried and failed several times to get her key into the lock. She finally got it inside on the fifth try, and Heather backed out of the drive to head to the Cambridge Flower Market. She hadn't been there in over a year, but from what she remembered from her last trip there, the crowds were normally pretty chaotic, as many florists, grocery stores, and other vendors had the same inside information she had.

"You know what I heard, Ant?" He grunted in response to her question. "One of the vendors there is going to have the most drop-dead gorgeous lilies there . . . in color combinations I've never seen in my life. And I heard it through the grapevine that President Johnson is absolutely obsessed with lilies."

Ant didn't act very impressed by what she had to say, so she prodded him a bit. "Come on, big guy! This vendor was successful in breeding the first naturally growing rainbow lily. Do you know how groundbreaking that is?" Heather laughed and continued driving.

She looked out at the road, enjoying the freedom of driving without bumper-to-bumper traffic so early in the morning. As she thought about the hour-long drive ahead of her, a smile spread across her face, knowing at least one part of this important errand would be stress-free. And that was when she saw it—one lone raindrop falling on her windshield, then, even more, came down.

"You know what they say, Ant: *April showers bring May flowers!* I think this is a good sign for our outing today, don't you think?"

Her little friend whined in response; he was never a big fan of rainstorms. In fact, the thunder sounds absolutely terrified him. As a puppy, Heather would find him shivering underneath the bed during a thunderstorm, and he wouldn't come away from his hiding spot for at least an hour. But he seemed to feel comforted when Heather had sung "Rain Rain Go Away" in her soothing, angelic singing voice whenever Ant got spooked. That gave him the courage to come out and wait through the storms in her arms.

"Alright, alright. I know you don't like the storms, but I'm here to protect you if it gets worse. You know I wouldn't take you out in this unless it was important to me, and *this* is very important. I'm starting a new job soon, and this beautiful lily will set the tone for my time as the greenhouse director at Shellesby College. Aren't you excited for me?"

Heather sang softly along with the radio to keep Ant calm, and before she knew it, she found herself pulling into the Cambridge Flower Market's parking lot. She happened to find the last remaining parking spot, and she was grateful they'd gotten there in time to snatch it up.

"Now, all we have to do is fight the crowd to get my flowers for my desk! That shouldn't be too hard, right?" But as she looked at all the people heading toward the entrance, she realized the odds might be stacked against her.

The clock on her dashboard announced that it was 4:45 a.m. Of course, she already knew she wouldn't be the only one there after those lilies, but she'd hoped the entire flower community within driving distance wouldn't be in attendance. The huge crowd she saw dashed those hopes right away. Letting out a deep sigh, she grabbed the end of Ant's leash and stepped out of the vehicle. Luckily, the rain had stopped, so she didn't expect she'd have to chase down the little guy if he got surprised by a crash of thunder later.

As Heather walked with Ant toward the front entrance of the market, she could only get so far before they had to stop walking. Ten minutes before the doors opened, she had some time to kill and was delighted to see a familiar face standing nearby. She looked to her right and saw Sunny Thornton, the owner of Thornton Flower Company, as indicated by the logo on her T-shirt. Heather had visited her flower shop many times in the past few years because Sunny always procured the best selection of beautiful and rare flowers. It was obvious the florist was here for the same reason—to get some of those amazing rainbow lilies.

Heather waved wildly at Sunny to get her attention. "Fancy meeting you here! It's nice to see a friendly face." Heather stretched that compliment quite a bit because she rarely knew Sunny to be very friendly. In fact, Heather didn't know a single soul in the entire local flower community who had anything positive to say about Sunny. Irony aside, Heather still felt a little better that she was there.

As the crowd watched the iron gates with purpose, they finally slid open, and Heather almost felt like she was standing in line to get past the Pearly Gates of Heaven. All they needed was a blinding white light to welcome them to the Garden of Eden. Heather peeked around the crowd to see what was happening, and it looked like pandemonium! This was beyond the frenzy of Black Friday mega-sales in the toy department.

The hysteria right here reminded Heather of her European backpacking trip after her high school graduation when she went to the Running of the Bulls in Pamplona, Spain. In this version, the bulls represented everyone in attendance who wanted to get at the rainbow lilies, the same flower Heather had her heart set on buying. Maybe if she didn't get trampled in all the chaos, she'd get to walk away unscathed and adorned with the rainbow petals she'd envisioned in her dreams. She bent down to pick Ant up so he wouldn't get lost or hurt, and when she stood back up, the line to get in had finally moved.

On your mark, get set, go! Heather encouraged herself to get through the crowd of people quickly. She passed one vendor playing flower-themed songs, and she got tickled when she heard "Every Rose Has Its Thorn" playing from their small speakers. One lady ran past them with her purse flying behind her, and it almost knocked Ant right out of Heather's arms. Heather gasped and moved out of the way, trying to find a much less violent path to the vendor.

When she finally got away from the cluster of people, she saw the vendor she was looking for, but several people crowded around that vendor waiting to snatch up the rainbow lilies. "Not on my watch!" Heather whispered, then continued walking forward. Then something happened that almost seemed like it was from a movie—a loud alarm bell sounded, and security guards descended on Heather.

Heather looked all around in confusion. "What's going on? What did I do?"

One of the guards grabbed her arm to escort her out of the market, then as they made their way to the gate, they brought a crowd of people with them. As the crowd moved farther away from the vendor, Heather looked back to see that it was completely empty now. She tried to wiggle her way out of the crowd and run back, but the security guard pulled her back.

"It will only take me a few minutes! Please! I really, really need to get some flowers!" Heather yelled.

"I'm sorry, ma'am," the officer growled, "but we have to secure the premises. Someone has set off the fire alarm."

A tall, good-looking gentleman in a designer suit scooted next to Heather, laughing. "Boy, you really *do* love flowers, don't you?"

Heather let out a deep sigh and shook her head. "I just . . . had my heart set on getting those flowers. I was so close! Now, I'm pretty sure the opportunity has passed. I'll never get those flowers now."

"What makes you so sure?" he asked.

Heather turned around and looked at all the people crowding together now in the parking lot. "Just look at all these people! They probably came for the exact reason I did. Don't you think?"

"And what is your purpose on this beautiful spring morning?" he asked.

"The rainbow lilies." As soon as Heather said it out loud, she realized her estimation was probably right—there was no way she'd get her hands on a bunch of those beautiful flowers now.

The man laughed. "I guess you're probably right. That's why I'm here too. My mother's birthday is coming up, and I wanted to surprise her with something rare and beautiful. I'd say it's a funny coincidence, but I suppose it's not a coincidence at all. The vendor *did* do a lot of marketing to the flower community for the past several months."

"Today is my first day as the greenhouse director at Shellesby College, and I wanted to impress the president. She loves lilies, and I thought the rainbow lilies would be a great icebreaker on my first day." Heather set Ant down on the ground now that they were in the parking lot with everyone else. He spread out on the cool pavement and shut his eyes for a bit of a nap.

A huge smile spread across the man's face, and he let out a laugh. "How funny! I work in horticulture too! What a small world." He extended his hand and introduced himself. "Lars Oslo at your service, director of the horticulture department at Middleton University in Boston."

Once he let go of Heather's hand, she took a step back to get a good look at him. He reminded her of a young Clint Eastwood, and she felt her face getting hotter the longer she looked at him. "It's nice to meet you, Lars," she somehow managed to say. "Heather Moore."

Suddenly, a light went off in Heather's mind as she sat there unable to look away from Lars. "Wait a minute! Your name sounds familiar. Are you the guy from last month's cover of *Botanical Digest*?"

The alarm stopped briefly, and they both looked toward the entrance. Several firefighters ran inside the market with their equipment right before the alarm went off again— louder and more agitating than before. Ant suddenly perked up, getting spooked at the loud noise. Heather had put her guard down and didn't have a strong hold on the leash anymore, so he slipped right out of her grasp. Before she knew it, Ant took off running on his little frantic legs that were determined to get away from all this noise.

Not giving Lars another second of her attention, Heather took off running to find Ant. Once she got into a wide-open space, she stopped to calm herself, looking all around to see where he headed off to, but her little guy was nowhere to be found. Now, panic struck her, and she ran to her car to see if he was hiding there. Still, she saw no sign of him.

Heather dropped to the ground immediately to look under her car because he sometimes liked hiding under there. Still, no Ant. Rolling over to check under the other vehicles, her hopes were dashed yet again. This day had turned out to be a complete disaster!

She jumped up, hitting her head against her side mirror in the process, and she rubbed her head to soothe the pain of the sudden impact. A little pain wouldn't slow Heather down when her most favorite thing in the world was missing. "Anthurium!" she yelled to get his attention. "Where are you?"

A group of people walked past Heather, and she stepped in front of them. "Have you seen a little Chihuahua running around here? He got away from me, and I can't seem to find him!"

They all looked at each other, shrugged, then shook their heads. "I'm sorry. We haven't seen your dog," one of the women said. "We'll keep an eye out for him."

Though she felt a little dejected and overwhelmed, Heather kept searching for Ant until a hush fell over the area after the firefighters turned off the fire alarm. That was when she heard it—his funny little bark that almost sounded like a turkey call. It was unmistakable—that was Ant!

She looked all around, then suddenly saw him high on top of a steep hill she knew she'd never be able to climb. Heather ran to the bottom of the hill and called up to reassure him. "I'm here, Anthurium! And I'm going to save you, no matter what it takes." She looked back at the main road and saw a line of firefighters headed to their truck.

"No, you can't leave! I need your help!" As Heather yelled, she ran toward the firemen as the last one was about to step onto the truck. "Please! Please! You've got to help me! My dog is stuck up on that tall hill!"

The young firefighter followed Heather's finger and squinted to see the little guy bouncing around on top of the hill. He looked like he was having the time of his life, but Heather knew he was more nervous and frantic than playful.

"Please!" Heather begged the fireman again. "He's my entire world! I can't lose him."

"Okay, okay, okay. We'll help you." The young man put his hand on Heather's back to calm her. "Don't worry. We'll get him down in no time."

Heather watched as they drove their truck around the block to get to the bottom of the hill, then she ran like crazy to get as close as she could. They extended the ladder up to the top of the steep hill, and the young firefighter climbed up to retrieve Ant. From where Heather stood, she could see him shaking like a leaf. Tears fell down her face upon realizing how scared he was.

Once the firefighter got back down the ladder with Ant, he jumped out of the young man's arms and into Heather's, then licked her face all over and wagged his tail. He was no longer shaking out of fear—now, he was just happy to be back with Heather.

"I'm *so* over this place, big boy! What do you say we get

the heck out of here?" Heather finally let out a deep sigh of relief and thanked the firefighters for their help. She held on tight to Ant as she walked as quickly as she could toward her car. There were more important things in life than getting her hands on some beautiful flowers, and she was grateful to learn that lesson with no harm befalling her best friend.

As Heather went to step inside her vehicle, Lars came running up to her. When he finally caught his breath, he revealed that he was holding two large bunches of the rainbow lilies.

"What's this?" Heather asked.

"You'd be proud of me!" Lars handed one of the bunches to Heather. "I fought off the crazy flower people and got the last two bunches of lilies."

"You did this for me?" Heather felt blown away by Lars' kindness. *Good-looking? Check! Funny? Check! Kind? Double check!* She tried hard not to let him worm his way into her heart, but she couldn't deny he had broken down at least one of her walls with this gesture. "You're kind of saving my day!"

"Ah, it's nothing. Those firefighters really saved your day. I'm just happy if I can make it a little better. The pot of gold at the end of the rainbow, if you don't mind the pun." He laughed and handed her his business card. "Will you email me later and let me know how it goes with your president? I'd love to stay in touch!"

Heather said nothing. She simply took the card and beamed at him as he turned to leave. She stared at the beautiful flowers, taking in everything that had happened that morning. Then Ant barked and pulled her out of her trance. *Yes, it is certainly going to be a great day,* she thought, then hopped into the car with Ant, and drove to the campus.

❉───🦇───❉

"AH, HERE WE ARE, ANT! NOTHING BEATS THIS GORGEOUS campus!"

Heather drove the sedate fifteen miles-per-hour speed limit along the narrow road that ran through the swanky Shellesby campus. She saw pathways lined with old-fashioned lights with lanterns hanging from them giving the affluent Ivy League College an air of gracious times past. English aristocratic elegance marked the layout of the sprawling campus, which lacked no expensive amenities.

Continuing through the heart of the college, she turned to her little dog and said, "We are now driving by Benefactors Hall, the oldest structure on campus, built by the first donors to the college in 1824."

Ant responded with a wag of his tail.

Heather looked out the window to the right and saw the imposing stone structure completely plastered with ivy vines growing up the side of the Hall, reaching to the sky. "Did you also know, Ant, that it has a carillon at the very top of the bell tower?"

Ant cocked his head to listen to the notes audible even through the car's window.

Described as the largest musical instrument in the world, a carillon typically has dozens of bells at the top of a tower. This carillon was the finest she had ever heard, the bells seemingly spanning three octaves of notes, expertly played by a very alert student, given the early hour.

"I wonder how much coffee that musician drank already today?" Heather laughed. "Did you know that a person playing the carillon is called a carillonneur? What a great word to use for trivia games!" Multitudinous notes fluttered out the very tiptop of the carillon, heralding a Baroque-era busy little piece of music, all played at breakneck speed by a very accomplished musician.

As she drove past the carillon, Heather dialed up Holly from her Bluetooth speaker and waited until she answered.

"Hi, Heather! Good morning . . . well, as much of a good morning as this can be with the downpours."

"Good morning, Holly! I think I see this cloud moving by, and hopefully, we will see a nice sunrise soon. How is everything going? Is everybody there?"

"Oh, we have a packed room waiting for you! The excitement is building. Everyone is waiting for you to arrive."

"Great news! I'm almost there. Meet me at the door."

"Sure thing! See you soon."

Heather drove a few more minutes to the east and pulled her electric car into her assigned director's parking spot in the lot adjacent to the greenhouse complex.

"Ok, Ant, here we are! Boy, am I glad that I brought that Thermos of coffee with me. I could sure use it after all the excitement of the morning." Heather got out and opened the door for her little dog.

With Ant eagerly stretching his legs, Heather became absorbed in observing the steam tendrils curl above her beloved morning blend in the Thermos she cradled in her hands and inhaled deeply, savoring the rich aroma. Her gaze shifted to the fog rising from the far side of the lake at this early hour. She saw the first raspberry rays of the sun illuminate the sky, their vivid colors reflected in the perfect mirror quality of Lake Tupelo's placid water.

Gentle splashing sounds alerted her to the presence of The Missus, the mate of Big Guy, two swans she had informally named when she was here a year ago for her reunion. Heather pointed her finger and showed Ant the swans. "Ant, is this the first time you've seen swans? I bet it is! Back in Washington, D.C., I don't ever remember seeing swans on our walks by the water. Oh, and look! There are ducks out there too."

Heather squinted closely and realized that The Missus had apparently gotten on the business end of a fishing line, and her foot had caught it and now was rendered useless, tucked up as it were on her back, producing a more awkward swimming form than her mate. She was diving rhythmically down into the water to eat her vegetarian breakfast of algae and other water weeds that grew bountifully in Lake Tupelo.

She scooped up her tiny dog, stroked his fur, and gave herself over to the scene, marveling at the stunning dual images of color—the sky and the mirror reflection of it on the lake. The lake's circumference was 2.2 miles and, at this hour, was deserted. Lake Tupelo was a favorite of dog walkers and joggers and poets and sensitive souls, all looking to immerse themselves in that little piece of heaven.

"Have you enjoyed this little time-out here with the sunrise? What a wild morning you had, Ant! I was so worried about you. Please don't ever take off like that again. I might not find you next time, and that would crush me," Heather said in heartfelt earnestness.

Ant wagged his tail and made a few noises in complete agreement.

The sunrise completed, that perfect blip in time now over, Heather focused her mind back on the matter at hand and walked up the path to the greenhouse complex with Ant.

Just then, Holly Jackson came bursting through the Visitor's Center door, resplendent in a beautiful pink dress and an ear-to-ear smile, followed closely by William Smith.

"Heather, it is so great to see you again!" Holly launched herself at Heather and gave her a heartfelt hug. Heather smiled as she remembered how Holly had been a rebel in her early years at Shellesby. Too much talent and unfocused energy had her getting into one scrape after another, but she was glad those difficult years seemed far behind Holly now.

She had helped mentor Holly through her growing pains, and by now, she almost felt like an aunt to her. She and her boyfriend, fellow brilliant botany expert William, were now employed at the college, and Heather knew she would enjoy their upbeat energy in the greenhouse.

William went immediately to her, leaned in for a quick hug, too, and immediately bent down to pick up Ant. "Ant! What a great surprise today. Are you taking over Heather's meetings and responsibilities already?"

"Oh, William, before I forget, I have a bundle of flowers on my passenger's side seat that need to go into my office. Would you mind taking those flowers to my office and getting Ant situated there so he can take a nap? I didn't want to leave him alone so long in the new house."

William was twenty-six years old and had recently graduated with a double doctorate at Shellesby in both horticulture and botany. He was a prodigy and had already made a name for himself in the plant world as a teenager when he was regularly written up in *Botanical Digest* for his groundbreaking inventions in the horticultural field. Now a prized acquisition of the horticulture department at Shellesby, he would be working closely with Heather in the greenhouses. He had a bright future, and Heather knew he hoped to run a major botanical garden organization himself one day.

A true Southern gentleman, he and Holly were inseparable and bonded over everything from plants to puppies. He had found a small cottage right next to the campus that was available to rent, which he called his Cot', and Heather knew Holly and William were more than happy and content there with their rambunctious beagle, Sweetpea.

"William, can you also please put those flowers in my car in a beautiful vase and in water? Please put them on my desk. I want to impress President Johnson later in my office. Those flowers will do the trick! I will have to tell you the harrowing story of my trip to the Cambridge Flower Market today.

Yikes! We had more trouble by 5:00 a.m. than most people have in a year."

"Sure thing! I'll retrieve them and then lock your car. I'll catch up with both of you as soon as I can." William smiled at Holly and Heather and turned to leave.

"Well, we better go in, Heather! The buzz is unimaginable already. Let's go!"

Heather opened the door to the greenhouse and was immediately taken aback by the rousing welcome she received. The Visitor's Center meeting hall was filled to capacity with the most wealthy donors from the last year. They were all alumnae who came solo or with their partners and were proud to donate to their alma mater to keep Shellesby at the forefront of botanical innovation and progress. As the new director, she was in charge of this annual open house to share with the donors updates on the progress the complex had made in the past year. A sea of smiling faces and loud applause enveloped her as the vice president of the college stepped forward and shook her hand.

"Ladies and gentlemen, may I present to you the new director of horticulture at Shellesby College, Ms. Heather Moore."

"Thank you for such a warm greeting! I know we all share a deep love for this special school, and I am determined to build on our illustrious past and maintain our standing as one of the top greenhouse complexes in the world!" Heather beamed at the assemblage and felt herself grow an inch taller as she felt the mantle of responsibility descend on her. No one loved Shellesby more than Heather, and she was going to guide it to even greater heights.

"As you know, we rely on your very generous donations each year to help us acquire the many rare plant species we have. We also use your funds for building improvements and upgrades, and I know you will be delighted to see what your monies have wrought for this year.

"I'm thrilled to lead you on a tour of the greenhouse now, and as the rooms are a bit small for the awesome turnout we had this morning, we will take you in groups through the rooms. William Smith, our resident genius master horticulturist, will accompany me with the first group, and Holly Jackson, my former standout student, will serve some of her mouthwatering cinnamon rolls and hot chocolate to those that will wait for the next tour. If you'd like to please follow me, I can take twenty of you now, and we will start by entering the Orchid Room to the left. Follow me."

Heather's face felt sore from smiling so widely because this was the highlight of her career; she had been waiting for this moment all her life. To have it come to pass and show off the greenhouse complex as the director of the department made her professionally satisfied on a very deep level, and she thought she never smiled as big as she did right now. She was also very happy that William returned from her office right in time to join her on the tour.

She led the group to a screen door and held it open as they passed through and into the Orchid Room, which had a hundred orchid plants displayed throughout, both on tables and in trees planted in soil in the middle of the display room. The trees were set off by a low stone wall, and there was abundant Spanish moss hanging from their branches as well. She pointed out huge white orchids almost four inches across and tiny deep red orchids in small pots. There were lime green orchids, pink ones, and an entire section of purple orchids.

"William, would you like to tell us about these orchids?" Heather asked.

"My pleasure, Director Moore! Please turn your attention to this exquisite plant over here. This is commonly called a dangling yellow chain orchid. I led the expedition to Borneo and the Philippines, and we sourced two dozen of them from the best growers there. They are quite picky plants and need a lot of care that includes high humidity."

"I can attest to the high humidity!" one donor called out with her hand up. "I want you to know that I spent a whole hour straightening my hair this morning to look great for this event and look at what I've become now!" She gestured amusingly at her head, where her naturally curly hair had exploded almost two feet out from her head in an abundance of frizz.

"And look at me!" Another donor chimed in. "My glasses fogged up." The pretty donor took her glasses off to wipe them on her sleeve.

"Yes, that is an occupational hazard here at the greenhouse. I feel I should get a bonus with my salary just so I can pay for the hair gel I go through every week." The crowd chuckled as handsome William put a hand up to his head and gingerly patted his hair in place. His hair had a gorgeous light brown hue that looked soft and shiny. The bright sunlight flooding the room made his warm toffee-brown eyes sparkle, and his easy smile revealed perfect teeth.

"I'll see about that bonus for you." Heather laughed and pointed out the rows of large, unusual-shaped orchids on a table next to the emergency exit. "Did you know that there are more than 20,000 orchid species in the world?" Heather told the group. "One of my favorite memories of seeing wild orchids was when I visited Machu Picchu in Peru and saw wild orchids growing amongst the ruins. Of course, they were thriving because the humidity was off the charts up there, as they are in a cloud forest environment with a potent rainy season. Humidity was sky-high, for sure. I wish I had better news for you, but the humidity is only going to keep climbing higher as we show you our Fern Room. Please follow me."

William held open the screen door at the far end of the room, and everyone streamed into the Fern Room. There was a lovely indoor small waterfall cascading into a small lily pond in the center of the room. Huge Australian tree ferns, twenty-feet-high and fifteen-feet-wide, populated the room and created a tall forest of ferns. Ferns were hanging in baskets from the roof and overflowing pots were on the tables lining the window.

There was a small hissing noise, then a fine mist started to drift down on the group. Everyone looked up in wonder.

"Yes, as promised, your hairstyles will take a further nose-dive, as we need to keep a constant mist on in this room so our prized ferns don't dry out. We water them, naturally, twice a day with both handheld hoses, and there are sprinklers on the ceiling, as you can see." Heather pointed skyward, and a sprinkler system could be seen on the roof of the greenhouse. "The other reason it is so warm in here is that the greenhouse has double-paned windows to keep out the bitter Boston chill during the winter. I hate to inform you, but it is 100 degrees in here at the moment because the May sun is quite potent, and we have had a string of over 80-degree days last week."

"Yes, I do feel like I am in the midst of a tropical jungle right now!" A donor fanned herself wildly with her bejeweled hand. She had on expensive rings and a tanzanite tennis bracelet.

"And check out this hair update!" the lady who had major frizz chimed in again. It did indeed look like her hair was even more wildly unkempt than it was only five minutes ago in the Orchid Room. Everyone chuckled.

"We went to Tasmania for these Australian tree ferns. They were sourced from local growers, and we hired a botanist to accompany them on the way back over to our college. It was a very expensive endeavor, but I am studying them in my lab here as they have astringent properties. I have had early success with using that astringent to provide anti-bacterial benefits, and I am currently doing further tests to see what else I can discover about the ferns. Again, you can see by this example how beneficial your donation dollars are. Tangentially, you are helping us test and explore medicinal benefits that could be game-changers in the medical field. Thank you for your continued support of the greenhouse complex here at Shellesby!"

William's words were greeted with thunderous applause that sounded even louder than it normally would due to the confines of the glass structure they were gathered in. Heather beamed at him with pride because she knew she could always count on William to be the darling of the donor population. As it was, they were crowding around him as he pointed out the many Boston ferns and staghorn ferns hanging from the baskets.

"Ladies and gentlemen, we hope you are properly warmed up," Heather joked as she headed the group to the far door and held it open for everyone to pass through.

"You've seen the rest, now see the best! This is the grand opening of our most treasured room in the complex. May I present to you the brand new Butterfly Room?"

Everyone streamed in through the doorway, which had a powerful burst of air constantly blowing.

"As you can see, this is a reverse airflow vent. We need to keep that on, or else the butterflies could fly out any time the door is opened. So, this is for their safety and protection."

Gasps could be heard as the group took stock of its surroundings.

A hundred butterflies of all species gently floated around this greenhouse room, making it a magical experience. Large green malachite butterflies gently swooped down and around the dozens of butterfly bushes and sunflower plants. Marigolds, black-eyed Susans, and a multitude of milkweed overflowed the display in the center. A gigantic mass of yellow bougainvillea dominated the room, and there were hibiscus, plumeria, and every variety of ginger plant.

"Does anyone think the shell ginger is a good flower as

the official flower for our college?" William asked with a grin. The applause that followed gave him his answer. "Yes, the founders thought so, too, and that is why it is our school flower!"

Huge swallowtail butterflies floated by the group, along with orange monarchs and the gigantic blue morpho butterfly.

"This spectacular room came about because William noticed that we already had the requisite bushes and flowers to create a butterfly haven, and he just suggested we go all out and look into creating a Butterfly Room. This room is very special, and as part of the outreach that Shellesby likes to do with the community, every fourth grader in West Shireston's four elementary schools gets to take field trips here once a week to experience the joy and wonder of this magical place."

"Exactly, Director Moore. We are indeed so proud we can share this with the community and spark interest in the natural sciences with these kids. Again, we can't thank you enough for helping us fund all these amazing events here at the college. Your support truly benefits many in our community. I know when Holly and I lead the kid tours here in the Butterfly Room, we hear from at least fifteen kids each time that they vow they are majoring in the natural sciences when they go to college. That would be great, as the field needs all the talent it can get."

The donors heartily applauded this speech as well, and Heather ushered them back out the door to the Tropical Jungle Room. "Ok, everyone, let's do one more room, and then we will have to go. I haven't even had time to fully browse this next room myself. I only recently moved back here from a decade of living in Washington, D.C. This is our Tropical Jungle Room."

Heather had no sooner led everyone inside and the screen door gently closed behind her when she heard a terrible sound. Water started shooting from the jets at the top of the roof.

"Oh, no! Let's go back to the Butterfly Room quickly!" Heather gasped in horror as the water rained down from the roof. She remembered she had told Holly to turn off the automatic timers so no one would get wet. The Tropical Jungle Room received the most watering per day, as those plants in there were used to soaking rains in their jungle environments.

Heather tried to summon her patience with Holly's obvious blunder. "William has run to turn them off. I am so sorry! We planned on turning off the automatic timers, and I guess that detail slipped through the cracks today in all of the excitement."

"Well, I'm already dry," said one donor's husband, rubbing his bald head and laughing.

"I'm so sorry this tour has gone roots up," Heather said sincerely. "I think we had our April showers allotment for the whole month just now. Please follow William as he accompanies you to our Athletic Complex to dry off. We have shower facilities where you can dry your hair. Afterward, enjoy a free breakfast on us at the Open Table!"

The group looked quite mollified, and smiles took the place of frowns as Heather continued smoothing over this unintended fiasco.

"Yup, the Open Table just won a culinary award from Boston Dining Magazine for its fresh organic delicacies! You'll love the space—it takes up the entire fifth floor of the Resources Building, with large floor-to-ceiling windows over-looking Lake Tupelo. It is open to the public, as well as the students and faculty, naturally. Here, let me search the day's menu for you."

Heather carefully extracted her cellphone that had luckily remained dry in her handbag and typed quickly on it.

"Ahhhh, here we are. They say this morning's omelet du jour is a fresh tomato and chive egg fantasy with a spoonful of dill-laced sour cream topping. The fresh juice bar features fresh-squeezed orange, pineapple, apple, pear, and straw-berry lemonade, along with a large selection of coffee blends, hot chocolates, and teas. Fresh danishes, exotic fruit salad, and a waffle and pancake station accompany favorite brunch items like Eggs Benedict, house-made nut butter, and freshly baked bread to toast. Finish them off with our Shellesby College berry jams, made right from our berry gardens," Heather finished with a dramatic flourish.

"Wow, wow, wow," said a donor and her husband in unison, their eyes gleaming in anticipation of a culinary blowout.

"Can I volunteer to be drenched every day, if it means breakfast at the Open Table?" said the lady who had complained about frizz all along. She looked tickled beyond belief at the thought of this upcoming epicurean feast.

Heather smiled and said, "At Shellesby, we always strive to exceed expectations, and we hope the memory of a huge breakfast banquet will erase the April showers experience!"

"Please take care, everyone! I have to go now as this is my first day on the job as director of horticulture here, and I believe the college president, Ms. Dahlia Johnson, is due to meet me in my office any minute. William will guide you the rest of the morning. Take care and . . . bon appétit!"

Heather waved at everyone as she turned right and walked five feet to a screen door, pulled open the door, and was immediately overwhelmed by the smell of mint and basil. A class was growing these herbs in one of the smaller greenhouses. There were tiny pots filled with the fragrant plants, all lined up like sentinels in a small army of plants occupying one of the many tables. Walking briskly through this student nursery, she passed by bags of half-opened and half-spilled potting soil, dozens of seedlings with their roots dangling down, fertilizer bags, watering cans, spades, sticks, and trays. She almost got her foot caught in one of the coiled hoses lying about as she carefully navigated around bags of sand and gravel, shovels and hoes, until finally arriving at an open door leading to the hallway where her office was.

When she opened her office door, she got the surprise of her life when she saw that Ant had found the only paper towel roll in the entire room. He'd gotten half of the roll shredded and strewn about the room so far, and he was about to destroy the rest of it until he saw the disappointed look on her face.

"What in the world am I going to do with you, Ant? It's our first day, and you're already misbehaving!" She walked over to Ant and got on her hands and knees to start cleaning up his mess—until President Dahlia Johnson popped her head into the office to check on her. With a bunch of destroyed paper towels in her hands, she stood up and walked over to greet President Johnson.

"I'd shake your hand, but it appears I'm in the middle of a situation here," Heather said. "I'm so sorry! He's not normally this unruly. We've had a bit of an exciting day today."

Dahlia walked over to the scene of the crime, her long black hair swaying back and forth as she did so. She crouched down in her six-inch heels to take in Ant in all his trouble-making glory. She ran her hand over the top of his head and smiled. "Ah, don't worry about it. This little guy reminds me of the little dog I had as a teenager. She was a spitfire too!" Ant licked her hand and wagged his tail to greet her.

When she stood up, her eyes latched onto the rainbow lilies, and her smile got even bigger. "My, my! These are exquisite. How long did it take you to dye these petals?"

Heather walked around to the flowers. In all the excitement, she hadn't gotten the opportunity to admire their natural beauty until now. They looked like something out of this world, and she blushed slightly at the memory of the handsome gentleman who had made her day much brighter than the colors on those petals. "They are actually not dyed. I found them at the Cambridge Flower Market this morning. There's a vendor there who's spent a decade trying to grow a rainbow lily naturally, and this is the result."

Dahlia leaned in to smell the lilies. "That's incredible! You *must* tell me where I can get some of my own! Quite honestly, I can't seem to stop admiring their beauty."

Heather beamed, proud her near-disastrous trip to the flower market had been successful. "Of course! I'll email you the details this afternoon."

After Dahlia left the office, Heather breathed a huge sigh of relief. "You naughty boy! I could have gotten into such trouble for your little mess here!" She continued cleaning up Ant's mess, then finally sat down at her computer to fire up her email. She wanted to shoot off some thank-you emails to the donors from this morning before it slipped her mind.

LATER THAT NIGHT, HEATHER SAT IN FRONT OF HER LAPTOP AT home and opened her email. She pulled out Lars' business card and kept looking over the words "Middleton University Horticulture Director." When she'd read the article on him in *Botanical Digest,* she pictured him much differently. She thought he would be an older gentleman with his nose turned up because of his long and prestigious career as an Ivy League professor. Middleton had a long and exciting history of cultivating the top greenhouse in the country, rivaling the best in the world.

She looked down at Ant who lay sleeping by her feet. "He didn't seem stuffy, snobby, or privileged at all." Heather didn't want to admit to it out loud, but she had been wildly attracted to the man. Not only was he one of the most handsome men she had seen in ages, but he probably forgot more about plants and flowers than she'd ever learned in her life. And she couldn't deny how intimidating that made him.

"What does he want with me, anyway?" she mused. "I'm just little old me—Heather Moore, the new director of Shellesby College's greenhouse." She beamed at how delightful those words sounded when she spoke them out loud, then repeated them over and over until she launched into a giggling fit over her silliness.

Then, as she stared at her computer screen, she brought herself back to the task at hand, suddenly growing a bit nervous about contacting the man. She typed in Lars' email address and started writing.

TO: Lars Oslo
FROM: Heather Moore
SUBJECT: What a day today has been!

Before I get into my day, I wanted to thank you for your kindness today. I was a stranger before today, and you really went out of your way to make my day better. I am truly grateful for that.

My first day went pretty well, I think, despite all the chaos. Trust me—you haven't heard all of it! When I arrived on campus, I got reacquainted with my old stomping grounds, and I have to admit that I'm still blown away by its beauty. Shellesby will forever hold a huge piece of my heart because of everything I've learned there, all the friends I've made, and all the memories that still make me smile today.

After meeting with our donors at our annual event for them, I went back to my office so excited and feeling positive about my future there. And when I opened my door—BAM! Ant had destroyed almost an entire roll of paper towels. It's almost like he was trying to embarrass me, because not a minute later, the president came walking in! Can you believe it? I was so mortified!

Luckily, she loved the little troublemaker, and I think the rainbow lilies made her forget about the intrusion. She absolutely fell in love with them. Thank you so much for making that possible!

But that's enough about me and my whirlwind of a day. Tell me. I must know! Did your mother love the flowers? I bet she went crazy when she saw them!

It's getting late, and I have an early morning tomorrow, so I'll sign off for now. Looking forward to hearing about your mother's birthday.

Regards,
Heather Moore

TWO

Heather had spent so much time focused on her new job ever since she moved into her family's estate that she didn't have a chance to explore the rest of the house. Though it had been a tradition for her and Ant to snuggle up together and watch the Boston Marathon on Patriots' Day every year, she decided reconnecting with her family was much more important.

As she looked around at her new home, she realized she'd forgotten so much about what felt so captivating as a child. With more than 4,000 square feet, her grandparents' old home had more space than any other home she ever lived in so far. In the main part of the house, she had her master bedroom, two bathrooms, the living room, and the biggest kitchen she could have ever dreamed of having. But there was so much more to this estate she now called home.

Heather walked down the hallway, and Ant followed obediently, practically dancing around in circles as he did so. He eventually pulled ahead of her and disappeared around the corner, and she thought there was no harm in letting him explore for a while. After all, he'd need to get used to living in such a sprawling house—some might say mansion. After she flipped on the hallway light, she found herself rocking back and forth in front of a door that held so many memories—her grandfather's office. It was the place where she spent so much time with Papa as he told her story after story about his adventures in the Republic of Botswana, a place he loved returning to year after year.

Releasing a deep breath, Heather pushed the door to her papa's office open and stepped bravely into what felt like a sentimental time machine. She couldn't believe it—the entire room smelled like him, a combination of freshly mown grass, bananas, and cedar. It felt so overwhelming that she had to brace herself on his custom-designed oak desk strong enough to survive any natural disaster. After a brief moment of sadness, she let a grateful smile pass over her lips until her eyes met a photographed gaze she wasn't prepared to face— her brother, Marshall Moore.

Wow, I haven't thought about him in a long time—not since Oliver's graduation. As soon as she thought of her brother's son, the memory of the protective older brother she had grown up with simply wouldn't quit. He practically nagged her from the grave, making her feel guilty about how disconnected she'd become from the family.

"It's not my fault," she tried to explain to the old photo. "I couldn't exactly take a lot of time away from my career after you died." And she was right—she couldn't. Because if she had, what would she have had left? Several dead family members and a lackluster career? *No thank you. Besides, I'm doing just fine on my own.*

After Heather walked around the room for several minutes, she decided she had enough of memory lane and walked back out to the living room. She flipped on the television and tried watching the marathon on the screen, but it wasn't the same. All that guilt built up inside her, and before she knew it, she had her phone in her hands, dialing a phone number she hoped still worked.

The young man who answered the phone sounded too much like Marshall, but she tried to ignore the pain that tried to beat down the walls of her heart. As she held back her tears, she found herself saying the words. "Why don't you come to have breakfast with me, Oliver?"

It wasn't long before the young man stood on her doorstep, practically the spitting image of a much younger version of her Marshall. Her heart pounded as she pulled the door open wider to invite him inside to share breakfast, though, by this hour, it was more like brunch. "It's great to see you." A slight catch in her throat caught her off guard. *No, I can't cry—not in front of my nephew.* Besides, Marshall had died a few years ago, and she had spent plenty of time mourning his tragic death. She was starting her new life, and it was time to look forward, not back.

They walked into the kitchen quietly, and she had already laid out an impressive spread for them to devour: miniature quiches with spinach and artichoke, mushrooms stuffed with gourmet cheeses and bacon, fresh-baked sourdough bread that still radiated the warmth she had made it with, deep-fried deviled eggs, and strawberry waffles stuffed with cream cheese and chocolate chips that had already started to melt.

The unbreakable silence was hard to take. Every time Heather looked up at Oliver, she tried not to see the same blue, sparkling eyes of her brother that had begged her to reach out to him. Maybe after they ate, she'd find the words to break the awkward silence, but for now, they both dug into the incredible food she had put her entire heart into.

Between bites, she would catch Oliver looking back at her, and she couldn't help but feel guilt over the mess he'd created in his life. After Marshall's death, Oliver started skipping school at first, then eventually found his way into even deeper trouble through vandalism, getting into fights, and mouthing off to local cops. His name was well-known all around town because he couldn't seem to keep himself out of trouble. His last stint in juvenile detention lasted about a year, and thankfully, he had cleaned up his act since then. As Heather considered all he had gone through, it didn't surprise her one bit that he had problems finding and keeping employment. At least, that was what she had heard through other family members.

"Thanks, Aunt Heather. It's been a long time since I've eaten food like that."

Probably not since Marshall's death, Heather mused, then offered Oliver a genuine smile. She had to admit, though, that it had been some time since she made such a spread, even for herself. Lately, it made her feel a bit too lonely having to cook only for herself. So she didn't remind herself of the oneness of it all, she had started resorting to quick and easy microwave meals or take-out lately.

"Ah, don't mention it! I'm happy to have a brunch buddy for once." As she put their dirty dishes in the sink and rinsed them off, Oliver walked around the expansive kitchen, looking out at the acres upon acres of greenery that seemed to repeat into eternity. Though the estate's outdoor attractions had seen better days, it was still something special to behold.

Heather turned the water off, wiping her hands on a pristine kitchen towel that hung on a hook by the window. Walking out into the living room, she turned back to Oliver. "Why don't we look through some of these boxes? I made sure to label them, so they should be easy to sort." She pulled a few boxes from the stacks along the walls and brought them closer to the couch so they could browse through them without hurting themselves.

Oliver shrugged and dragged his feet along the carpet. "I guess so." He walked past Heather and approached the front door, peeking out to see the porch. "Looks just like I remember it. Say, what happened to those apple trees out front?"

Heather knew he didn't care about the apple trees, so she

tried to redirect his energy. "Why don't you come to sit by me? We can look through this old scrapbook of photos if you're bored." She grabbed the box with a label that read "photo albums" and pulled it closer to her. Her prized possession on the top of the box was a designer photo album she had purchased to hold all the memories from her sister's wedding she and Ant had attended in Maine the previous year. "Oh, look! These are from Aunt Shelley's wedding last year. Since you weren't there . . ." Heather immediately lost her train of thought once she looked up and saw the scowl painted across Oliver's face.

"Right," Oliver said as he glared at Heather, "we couldn't make it to the wedding. Been a long time since we could afford a vacation."

As Oliver's glare practically burned a hole through Heather, she knew he was saying more with his tone of voice than his words. His tone almost sounded accusatory, and she didn't understand where the attitude came from. She tried to ignore it and turned back to the photo album, though Oliver kept his death stare focused on her.

Opening the album to the first page, she saw a photo of her and Ant the photographer had taken for her. "Aww, look how handsome Ant was that day!" Heather tried to stay positive, even though the current situation felt rocky and unstable. She let her eyes focus on the photos in front of her, and she couldn't help but smile as she looked at her handsome little man in the pictures. He had been the ring bearer at Shelley's wedding, and he was dressed to the nines in his tiny canine tuxedo.

Oliver's eyes briefly fell to the photo of Ant, and he let out a derisive laugh. "I'll bet his outfit cost more than the shoes I'm wearing right now." He shook his head and let out a deep sigh. "Seems like such a waste when you have a family—"

Now, he had backed Heather into a corner by attacking

her beloved furry family member. "He's just as much a part of my family as you are, Oliver. What's with the attitude?"

Oliver turned away. "Just forget it. I know you don't care."

Heather got off the couch and walked over to Oliver, placing a light touch on his back to comfort him. "Oliver, I really do, or else I wouldn't have invited you here. Please. Tell me what's wrong. What's going on?"

Oliver turned around with a blank look on his face. "Can we talk about something else?"

Heather dropped her hand and smiled at Oliver. "Of course. Hey, I know! There's a room down the hallway I thought would be perfect for you. And you're welcome to come visit and stay here any time you like. How does that sound?" Whatever was bugging Oliver, Heather hoped this would make him feel better. Despite his sour attitude, she believed he had a good heart—he simply had a run of impossible circumstances to fight his way through. Maybe having his own space here would help him feel more connected to his dad's side of the family. And Heather wanted to do everything in her power to make him feel welcome.

Oliver shrugged and managed a half-smile. "Sounds alright."

Heather motioned for him to follow her, and they both walked down the hallway together. Time seemed to fly by as they spent some time clearing out a room for Oliver.

After about an hour, they made their way back to the living room to tackle the boxes. Oliver seemed to be in a brighter mood, and he even joked with Heather about the boxes upon boxes of kitchen utensils and food gadgets she rarely used these days. It was a good thing she had all those seemingly useless kitchen tools and appliances, though, because she felt as though her new kitchen was as big as her old apartment in Washington, D.C.

Box after box, they worked together in harmony now organizing belongings she hadn't seen in ages and putting them all away in their proper places. When they were halfway through what she wanted to accomplish for the day, Ant finally got bored of his exploring and made his way back into the living room, carrying a stuffed mouse toy that looked like it had been killed at least ten times. Heather kneeled to pick up the nasty thing and shook her head.

"Looks like you found one of Pansy's toys! Maybe we'll just set that aside before you get any diseases from that smelly old thing." But where was Pansy? Heather had grown up around that old cat who never seemed to leave her papa's side, but ever since she moved into the estate, she couldn't find her. Heather inspected Ant to see if he'd gotten the business for stealing the old girl's toy, but he looked untouched. Maybe after lunch, she'd ask Oliver to help hunt her down. She had to be hiding in some secret nook or cranny.

"What? You have another dog?" Oliver asked as he moved some boxes around the living room.

"Oh, no. Pansy is Papa's cat. Don't you remember her?" Heather walked over to Oliver and helped him lift a rather large box. "She's so old I think she must be on her eighteenth life by now. The estate lawyer said that was the only condition of inheriting the house—that I'd need to take good care of Pansy. She was Papa's pride and joy for as long as I can remember."

"She was kind of mean, though, wasn't she? I swear, every time I came here as a little kid, she tried to scratch my eyes out," Oliver said. "Papa always said that was her way of showing affection. But I think she was just kind of a—"

"Shhh! She might hear you and exact her revenge!" Heather laughed. "I'm sure she'll turn up eventually, though."

After they moved the last box into the middle of the living room, Heather wiped the dust off her hands and headed into the kitchen. "I've worked up kind of an appetite this afternoon. What do you say to some lunch?"

As soon as she said *lunch*, Ant's head popped up, and he wagged his tail rather lazily while he lay next to a box on the couch. He half-barked, then rolled over and drifted back to sleep.

"Sounds good to me," Oliver said.

"Why don't you take those boxes over there labeled 'Winter Clothes' up into the attic for storage. I think it's warmed up enough this spring that I won't need them for a while." Heather turned and headed into the kitchen to start preparing lunch for both of them. She wasn't sure if she could top the amazing brunch they had earlier, but she was determined to give herself a run for her money.

"Oh, and Oliver?" When Heather looked back up to remind him to come back down for lunch, he was nowhere to be found. The only sign of Oliver that lingered was the sound of his footsteps above her head as he took the boxes up to the attic. Heather shook her head, then headed into the kitchen. She was sure he wouldn't be up there long, so she needed to hurry up and get lunch made.

Ant followed Heather into the kitchen, plopping down and enjoying the cold tile against his belly. With his head rested on the floor, he watched as Heather finished the dishes from brunch and made sure the kitchen was spotless before continuing.

"So, what do we think of Oliver? Hm?" Heather looked over at Ant, and he let out a soft whimper. "Yeah, I know. He's a bit rough around the edges, but he's family, okay? I expect you to be on your best behavior around him."

Ant wagged his tail as Heather spoke.

"I mean, better than usual." She went to work to make gourmet grilled cheese sandwiches for both of them, taking out some bacon, tomatoes, avocado, deli roast beef, Swiss cheese, and a carton of eggs. Adding a sunny-side-up egg was Heather's signature final touch; the yolk oozing onto the other ingredients added a richness that tasted heavenly.

Ant perked up when he heard the pan sizzle and smelled the aroma of the bacon. Heather always gave him a treat whenever she cooked, and it couldn't come soon enough!

"He's a really good kid, you know." Heather turned to look at Ant, waving the spatula at him as she talked. "All he needs is some love from Aunt Heather to push him in the right direction." Of course, she knew she couldn't solve all his problems for him, but she hoped she could at least make a difference in his life. She imagined Marshall looking down on them and smiling to see them working together as a family.

With her food preparation finished, Heather added the eggs to the sourdough bread slices leftover from brunch and put their oversized grilled sandwiches on two plates. Then she grabbed a couple of lonely bacon slices and offered them to Ant, who downed them practically without even chewing.

She walked to the bottom of the stairs to call up to Oliver. After yelling his name several times, Heather walked around the corner and stopped in front of the library when she heard some strange sounds coming from inside. She knocked on the door and called out to Oliver, hoping she'd find him inside, but he didn't answer back. Pushing the door open, she found the room to be empty, but she was amazed at how much the room had changed since she'd been to the estate last.

From the floor to the ceiling, she gazed in amazement at her grandfather's collection of horticulture and botany books he had thoughtfully arranged by year. His collection went back to the 1800s up to books that had been released as recently as two years ago. With how much time she spent at work, she thought it might be a good idea to use these books to start a departmental library she knew both undergraduate and graduate students could get some great use of for their research and personal enjoyment. She made a mental note to talk to Holly when she saw her next about heading up a memorial library named after her grandfather, Hudson

Moore. "The Hudson Moore Memorial Library. That has a rather nice ring to it."

Heather heard the strange noise again—it was coming from behind one of the middle bookcases in front of her. She approached that set of books cautiously and got the surprise of her life when it got suddenly pushed forward, knocking her down to the floor. Pansy came tearing through the opening, hissing, and scratching as she jumped onto Heather's back. Closely following behind her was Oliver, laughing and running through the room after the cat.

"Surprise!" Oliver yelled as he looked over at Heather, who was still stuck on the floor.

But by the time Heather pushed herself up, Oliver had taken off again, back through the secret opening in the library that presumably offered an alternative path up to the attic above her. She closed the door right away and took off running back to the staircase. "Oliver! Get down here right this instant! Lunch is ready!"

Before Heather could turn back and head into the kitchen, Oliver popped his head around the corner at the top of the stairs, still laughing and breathing heavily. She wagged her finger at him and shook her head. "Come on down before your lunch gets cold!"

After Oliver caught his breath, he walked over to the banister, straddling it, with his back facing Heather. "Geronimo!" he yelled as he pushed himself off. And before Heather could jump out of the way, he came careening down the banister, jumping off, and knocking her over again.

"You have a knack for knocking me down! And I don't appreciate it one little bit." If he kept this up, Heather would be in the hospital before she knew it, and she couldn't afford to miss any work at her new job. She felt lucky enough that she had this holiday off so she could get her new home in order, but life had to get back to normal soon.

"No need to get all bent out of shape, Aunt Heather. I'm

just having a bit of fun. You should try it sometime." Oliver helped Heather up from the wooden floor, then strolled into the kitchen to sit down for lunch.

"No, thank you. I think I've had all the excitement I can handle today. But on the bright side, you found Pansy, so I guess that's something." Heather shook her head as she followed Oliver into the kitchen.

After they both sat down at the table, Ant followed and lay on the floor next to Oliver's feet, probably hoping he'd toss him some bacon he could gulp down. Oliver picked at his sandwich but didn't seem like he had much of an appetite. He watched Heather closely as she took her first bite. "I found something kind of crazy in the library when I was in there."

"Oh?" Heather perked up. "What did you find?"

"It was a letter someone sent to Papa. They were threatening him because of his shady business practices. You know anything about that?" Oliver asked.

Heather glared at Oliver, upset he would even suggest such a thing. "You know, it's not nice to speak ill of the dead after they're gone. Besides, what could you possibly have against him? Papa always went out of his way to help everyone, and nobody ever had an unkind word to say about him. Why start making up stuff now, Oliver? I know you like drama, but—"

Oliver looked away from Heather. "I didn't make it up. Never mind. I guess it's not important."

Heather tried to remind herself that it was only one day out of many that she'd have to tolerate Oliver's shenanigans. *He'll be gone soon enough,* she reminded herself before she changed the subject entirely. "How are things going with you and Mary? I thought I saw a nice picture of you two recently on Instagram. You looked very happy," Heather said, setting her sandwich down to engage with Oliver.

Oliver shrugged and let out a sarcastic laugh. "They aren't

going. They aren't going at all. Ever since Papa fired her right before he died, she's been acting a bit strange."

Heather thought she saw a flash of anger in his eyes, and it concerned her. "Really? What happened?" She kept her eyes focused on him as he sat there and glared back at her—until she heard Ant growl at her feet. His growls kept getting loud and louder as he moved closer to Oliver underneath the table. The growling suddenly stopped and turned into a loud yelp and whining as Ant went scurrying out of the kitchen.

She stood up and ran after Ant into the living room, where she saw him limping as he approached the coach. Scooping him up gently into her arms, she caressed his fur softly and tried to calm him down. "Shh. Shh. It's okay. I've got you." Heather wrapped him in his favorite blanket and situated him in the corner of the couch.

Realizing what had happened, Heather went into mama bear mode and stormed into the kitchen, stopping right in front of Oliver. "What in the world was that for? My little guy didn't do anything to you! If you don't want me to kick you out of this house right now—"

Oliver stood up and backed away from Heather, putting his arms up in surrender. "Look, I'm sorry. It was an accident. I swear! I didn't mean to hurt him. Your question just got me off guard, okay? I'm a little peeved at my girl is all. It triggered me."

Oliver's words suddenly disarmed Heather, and she calmed down a bit. She walked over to Oliver and placed her hand gently on his back. "Well, what's going on? It could help to talk about it."

He shrugged and shook his head, then that look of anger returned to his face as he started ranting and raving about his relationship. "Look, I don't know why he fired Mary—she got mad every time I asked. But she cheated on me, okay? So, I broke up with her. She kept lying to me, saying she had to work late here with Papa, but I don't think that was ever true."

"I'd completely forgotten she worked for Papa." Then she frowned, feeling quite bad about the end of her and Oliver's relationship. "I'm so sorry it didn't work out between you two." Heather tried to disarm him by being kind, but he only got angrier as he spoke about his ex-girlfriend.

"How could she do that to me, Aunt Heather? I love her so much! And now . . . and now . . ." Oliver clenched his fists and looked like he was about to explode. "Now, I hate her. I couldn't care less about where she is or what she's doing or how she feels. That . . . she's . . . she's dead to me."

After finishing the remainder of the lunch in silence, Heather realized they had gotten a lot of work done in the house, and Oliver was still too angry to be of much help. She continued to try to help calm him down, but she could eventually tell he just needed to sulk alone with his thoughts. Though she extended an invitation for him to stay there that night, he said he needed to take care of some things back home but that he'd be in touch with her. As he left in a rush through the living room and out the front door, Ant lifted his head, growled at him, then went right back to sleep.

Heather looked up at the clock and realized if she didn't get started on her garden soon, she might not get an opportunity today. So, she took a few minutes to relax and check her email so she could clear her head after her visit with Oliver. She was delighted to find an email message from Lars waiting for her.

TO: Heather Moore
FROM: Lars Oslo
SUBJECT: Re: What a day today has been!

Wow, I can't wait to hear about everything that happened—in full detail—when I see you next. (I'm hoping there will be a next time!) I'm sure my day will sound pretty dull in comparison to yours, but Mom simply adored those rainbow lilies. We had a nice birthday lunch and spent the rest of the day going from nursery to nursery because she's been wanting to do some work in her garden this spring. Though, if I'm being honest, what she really wants is for me to re-do her flower garden! Between you and me, she doesn't have the greenest thumb, so I have to put in some work in her yard from time to time.

But what she loved more was hearing about you, to be honest. I told her I met this sweet, endearing beauty at the flower market, and she simply wouldn't stop asking me about you! Ah, you know how mothers are.

Well, I have an early morning at Middleton tomorrow, so I'm going to sign off for now. What do you think about us grabbing dinner sometime? I'd love to get to know you better, Director Heather Moore!

Heather closed her email and let the warm glow from his words fill her as she went to her bedroom to change clothes and head out to her garden.

THREE

With the inside of her new home mostly in order, Heather knew she'd have to tackle the overgrown garden soon. Since spring had just begun, there was no time like the present. Besides, it had been a long time since Heather did some serious work in her very own garden, so she was looking forward to tackling this huge project.

She stood in front of the mirror admiring her new gardening outfit as Ant danced all around her with the excitement of an outdoor adventure in the landscape. Pansy was starting to get used to Heather being around the house more, so she was there, too, rubbing up against Heather's feet.

A giggle passed through Heather's lips as she took in the vision of her standing there dressed in her new gardening overalls, an outfit reminiscent of the one her grandfather had given her as a child. She had planned to get dirty in these clothes, so she purchased them in a fine "dirt" color, knowing she wouldn't have to worry about unsightly stains at the end of the day.

"Alright, guys! What do you think? Am I ready to tackle this garden like a boss, or what?"

Both Ant and Pansy perked up, ready to go take care of some outside business of their own. Ant had some territories to mark, and Pansy grabbed her old mouse toy, ready to show it who was the boss of this house.

Heather stepped outside and reacquainted herself with Papa's old garden. She remembered how exquisite it had looked as a child, and it darkened her heart to see it as it was now, with overgrown weeds, dead rose bushes, and several varieties of plants that had become a quite tasty meal for several species of insects. A tear rolled down her cheek to see it in such a state.

Realizing she'd need some quality tools to tackle her garden project, Heather looked immediately to the shed a few feet away from the old garden. Her grandfather had normally kept a solid lock on the doors, but the padlock she remembered being there was nowhere to be seen. She didn't think anything of it, though, because she was sure plenty of people had come in and out of the estate since Papa's passing.

Heather wiped away the cobwebs as she opened the shed doors, then looked around for anything she could use to get to work on the garden. The entire shed almost looked ransacked, like some thief had broken into the place to do some undercover midnight gardening. After she sifted through a pile of old tools, she wandered across something that seemed out of place—a set of gardening tools that looked almost brand new and weren't covered by layers of dust like the other tools.

She flipped over the tools to see some words engraved on the metal handles, "Property of Thornton Flower Company." Heather didn't understand why Papa would have had those tools lying around in his shed, but then again, he normally had tools hanging around from all kinds of places, so it wasn't really *that* weird to see them there.

As she walked deeper into the shed, where her grandfather normally kept the larger tools, there was a faint smell of chocolate that invaded her nose. As soon as she smelled it, she forgot all about the garden and wondered if there was a secret stash of candy bars hidden somewhere in the shed. Heather looked in every nook and cranny she could think of, but she came up empty-handed. She let out a sigh of defeat. "What a shame! No chocolate for you, Heather," she said quietly to herself.

When Heather went to shut the last drawer she had opened in her frantic search for chocolate, something had created an obstruction, preventing her from closing it all the way. She tried to force it closed several times, but it wouldn't budge. Heather always liked her home to look organized and methodical, so she wouldn't get any sleep that night if she went all crazy and left a random drawer open like that. Next to the drawer, the cabinet had two large doors that swung open, so she grabbed onto the handle to investigate what the problem was. As soon as she pulled on the handle, an awful stench escaped the cabinet, one she'd never smelled in her life.

Heather stumbled back and hunched over, practically losing her lunch with Oliver all over the floor of the potting shed. With the foul odor now taking over, she ran outside to get some fresh air, taking several deep breaths in and out. Now, she had two problems: a drawer that wouldn't close and a horrible smell she'd never be able to get out of her pretty new gardening overalls.

Ant and Pansy walked by to investigate what had happened. As soon as Pansy stuck her head in the shed, she let out a monstrous hiss and ran as far away as she could. But not Ant. He was so interested in what caused the smell he went inside to sniff out the culprit. As soon as he got inside the shed, Heather freaked out, as if something bad would happen to him because of the smell.

"No, Ant, no! Stay out of there! You don't know what's in there! It could be a—"

But when Ant got the cabinet door open even farther, Heather saw exactly what it was, and she was right to be freaked out. It looked awfully similar to . . . *a . . . human hand? I must be having a nightmare!* Intent on saving Ant, she held her breath and ran in after him, her heartbeat rising and rising the longer she had to stay in the shed.

Heather scooped him up, ran back out, and gently placed him on the ground. She paced back and forth agitatedly in front of the shed, talking to herself. "It can't be a person, right? I'm sure I just imagined seeing a human hand in my shed!" Ant lay on the ground in front of the shed whining and watching Heather walk a worn path in front of the door.

She grabbed the door and opened it slightly to peek. *Yep. The creepy hand-like thing is still there. You need to be brave, Heather. Just get in there and see what it is once and for all! There's no possible way it could be a dead body.* So, Heather held her breath one last time and took one heavy step right after the other toward the cabinet. When she bent down to peek inside the cabinet, she saw even more of the obstruction—the gray eyes of someone who had met their unfortunate end on her grandfather's property. Heather let out the loudest and most frightening scream that had ever escaped her mouth, then shut the door behind her and ran to find the nearest phone.

With shaky hands, Heather gripped her cell phone as the 9-1-1 operator answered her call. "Yes . . . I . . . I think there's a dead body in my shed. No, I didn't kill them. No, I don't know who they are. Yes! Please send an officer right away!"

It didn't take long before Detective Huff arrived on the scene with two additional units to assist him in the investigation. As soon as Heather showed him where she had found the body, he got on his cell phone and arranged for a team of forensic scientists to help in the investigation. As soon as he saw a traumatized Heather step out into the area outside, he approached her to find out more information.

"I'm sorry, Detective, but I just moved into my grandfather's estate this week. So, I'm afraid I don't know much about whoever it is that's in that shed." She stopped and wiped tears away with a tissue.

An officer approached Detective Huff, and he nodded in the officer's direction. "Miss Moore, this is Officer Wilson. She's going to escort you to your room so you can grab some belongings. This investigation is just starting, and we're going to need you to stay elsewhere for the time being."

"Oh. I didn't think about that." Heather tried to smile, but she had nothing to be happy about. So, she followed Officer Wilson into the house, then led the way to her bedroom. Far enough away from the dead body, she felt like she could relax a little while she put together a suitcase of clothes. Once she finished packing, Officer Wilson escorted Heather to her car with Ant and Pansy in tow, and she handed her a business card.

"You're probably still in shock right now, but it would be best if you stay in touch. Detective Huff will want you to stop by the station sometime this week once he knows a little bit more about the case." Officer Wilson offered a gentle smile and walked back inside the house.

Heather opened the door to let her fur babies inside, then tossed her suitcase in the back seat. After she got inside and started her car, she only knew of one place she could go in her time of need. So, she picked up her phone and dialed.

"Hello?" William answered.

"Yes, William? Do you think I could ask a favor of you and Holly?" Heather looked over at the twosome sitting in her passenger seat and let out a deep breath. "I'm having some electric problems at the house, and I wondered if I could stay with you guys for at least a few days. I can't go to a hotel with Pansy and Ant, and I . . . I just don't know where else to go." Tears started falling down Heather's face, and she wiped them away. She knew she couldn't tell them the truth —not yet.

For now, she'd need to keep the dead body in her potting shed a secret. She summoned her inner strength and hoped she was not too distraught to drive. The sooner she could relax at William's Cot' and try to process this upsetting day the better.

FOUR

Right when Heather was about to pull out of her driveway and head to William's Cot', Ant pressed the down button on the passenger's side electric window, and it didn't even take a second for Pansy to take advantage of her opportunity to escape. Heather let out a deep sigh as she jumped out of her car. "I guess that's what I get for not putting you in your carrier to begin with." She quickly pulled the carrier from the car and took off running to corral Pansy.

They both darted down the neighborhood in a zig-zag pattern from house to house. Heather would get about an inch from Pansy, then she'd hiss and take off down the street again. This went on for several minutes until they ran into one of the biggest dogs Heather had ever seen—a Great Dane being walked by his owner. Though the man had this horse of a dog on a leash, Pansy didn't care. She growled and hissed her way back toward Heather, who took the opportunity to pop the door for the carrier open. This time, Pansy was more than happy to take a ride in the carrier.

Mentally drained and physically exhausted, Heather made the slow walk back to her car to get Pansy in there for good. By the time they returned, Ant had hopped into the driver's side and was trying with all his might to honk the horn, jumping up and down on the steering wheel. His dainty little feet weren't strong enough, though. Heather laughed and wondered if this was a sign of what was to come at the Cot'. *I sure hope not!*

Once Heather got inside the little cottage William and Holly shared, she placed Pansy's carried gently on the floor and practically collapsed on the couch. As William hovered over Heather to help, she shook her head and said, "Sorry, William. I just need a minute to relax before I do anything else. You wouldn't believe the day I've had!"

"No worries! Let me get Pansy out of her carrier for you, and then I'll grab you a fresh cup of tea—Holly just brewed a pot, especially for you." William popped open the carrier, and Pansy took off zooming around the room at full speed. He watched as she ran circles around the couch that would give any NASCAR driver a run for their money. Laughing all the way to kitchen, he returned quickly with a steamy cup of tea for Heather.

"Thank you! You don't know how much I need this right now." Heather closed her eyes and floated off into fantasy land for a moment now that she could finally relax.

Holly came running into the living room with a squeal of excitement. "Oh, I'm so happy you're here! We're going to have so much fun!"

William wrapped his arms around Holly and placed a soft kiss on her lips. "She's just coming to stay for a few days—not joining the circus. Let's give her a minute alone to enjoy her tea before the welcoming committee gets too out of control."

Before Holly and William shut their bedroom door, their beagle, Sweetpea, escaped quite stealthily so she could check out her new furry roommates. Pansy had finally stopped zooming around, and Sweetpea ran to take cover between Heather's legs because she seemed a little unsure of this new thing called a cat. Heather laughed and reached down to pet the beagle. "It's okay, girl. She won't hurt you."

Pansy approached Sweetpea from behind the couch, tapping her paw against her new friend's nose. Sweetpea jumped back suddenly, letting out a loud howl. Pretty soon, Ant ran over to see what was going on and joined in the chaos. He lifted his nose to the ceiling and tried to howl, but it was no use. He simply wasn't equipped with the skills for a proper howl. Instead, he sounded like a crying baby. While both Ant and Sweetpea continued to croon at each other, Pansy jumped up on the couch and snuggled next to Heather. That was, until Sweetpea lunged at Pansy, ran across Heather's lap, and chased the poor cat around the room.

When Pansy finally got enough distance between her and the dogs, she jumped up on the kitchen counter, over to the top of the refrigerator, and finally onto the chandelier. The chandelier swung back and forth wildly while Ant and Sweetpea danced around on the floor below trying to get at her. She hissed and growled, and she batted her paw in the direction of the troublemaking dogs to make sure they really couldn't get at her.

"Help! Help!" Heather called out as she chased Ant around the small cottage, but it was no use. She couldn't catch him.

William burst through the bedroom door to save the day with Holly trailing not far behind him. Holly took off after Sweetpea and wrestled her into her arms, petting her softly to calm her down. William was tall, but he still couldn't reach Pansy on the chandelier, so he took off to go find something he could use to rescue the poor thing.

As William approached Pansy with a step ladder, Heather stood in the corner watching as the feline acrobat calmed down. "I think she likes you! Took her much longer to get used to me."

Holly laughed. "We're going to have to add Cat Whisperer to your resume—right underneath Plant Rock Star!"

William laughed. "Oh, you know! The ladies just love me." As he carried Pansy into the living room, she nuzzled him and purred loudly against his chest. When he went to place her gently down on the couch, she let out a loud meow and dug her claws into him. "Guess I'm stuck with you for the night, Miss Pansy." Then he looked over at Holly. "I think Pansy might give you some competition."

——🐾——

AFTER A LEGENDARY DINNER OF STUNNING TOMAHAWK STEAKS; gourmet macaroni and cheese with Swiss, bacon, and mushrooms; and a rainbow orzo salad; Heather was feeling decidedly worn out after the long and stressful day. She plopped down on the couch and looked outside—it was still light out. "I can't believe it's still so early, guys. I'm not sure if I will last the night."

Holly jumped out of her chair with excitement and rushed over to Heather. "Oh no, you don't! I have a surprise for you that I think you are going to love. Then, afterward, we can have some of William's specialty: dark chocolate mousse!"

Heather perked up at the mention of dark chocolate. "Oh, goodness! Are you two looking for a permanent roommate? Because I could certainly get used to Casa de Cot'!"

Holly grabbed Heather by the arm and led her to the bedroom. She turned back before she shut the door and called out to William, "Think you can handle the furry children for an hour or so? Heather and I are going to have some quality girl time!"

William ran his hand over Pansy's silky fur. "I've got my number-one fan right here. I'll be fine!"

After Holly closed the door behind them, she ran into their master bathroom and called out to Heather, "Give me a minute for me to finish mixing my masterpiece, and we'll get started with the festivities." Heather tried to sneak up to see what Holly was doing, but Holly shut the bathroom door right away. "No snooping! I'm almost done," she called through the door.

The long, stressful day combined with the amazing gourmet meal was starting to take a toll on Heather. Her eyelids got heavier and heavier, but she knew she had to hold on a little bit longer. She closed her eyes to relax, though, and she couldn't help seeing those gray eyes again. The fact that somebody's son or daughter was lying in the morgue and she was here having a girl's night made Heather feel extremely hollow inside. She knew it wasn't right, but she didn't want to seem ungrateful to her amazing hosts. So, she tried to put it out of her mind. *It's just for one night*, Heather reminded herself. *Tomorrow, I can go back to stressing out about finding a dead body in Papa's potting shed.* She let out a deep sigh and opened her eyes.

Holly walked out of the bathroom, holding two bowls of a creamy brown substance. "You just lie back on the bed while I pamper you. I know you've had a long day, and I want to treat you to something luxurious."

"What in the world is that?" Heather asked.

"Just close your eyes!" Holly took a spatula and started applying a custom mud mask on Heather's face. As soon as the cold mud hit her skin, her body jumped. "Just relax. It might be cold at first, but it will feel relaxing here in a minute." As she continued applying the mud, she explained, "This is a mixture of nutrient-rich soil that comes from an area in Turkey that's known as 'The Fertile Crescent.' I've combined it with dried rose petals I procured from the Shellesby Greenhouse, passionflower oil William extracted for his research, and organic sunflower powder I purchased at the Boston Flower Market. I've been doing these once a week for the past few months, and even William has made comments about my glowing skin!"

"Wow!" Heather exclaimed. "That sounds—and feels —amazing."

"See?" Holly teased. "I told you it would! Now, we just need to let this soak into our beautiful faces for about ten minutes, then we can—"

A loud crash echoed throughout the Cot', and both Holly and Heather sat at attention. It sounded like pure chaos through the door with the menagerie of animals running around the living room and William yelling after them.

"Oh, no!" Heather ran to the door. "It sounds like William is getting taken over by the tribe." She swung the door open, and that was exactly what she saw. Ant ran around like crazy from corner to corner of the living room while Sweetpea bounded right after him, both of them barking up a storm as the chase continued.

William ran like a madman around the room with Pansy still hanging onto him for dear life.

"Every time I try to put her down, I fear for my life!" William screamed amid all the madness. "But it's cool! I have everything under control." Then, when he looked at Heather and Holly, he stopped abruptly, shaking his head. "Is this some kind of secret society ritual I'm not aware of?"

Both Holly and Heather exchanged confused glances.

"Uh . . . you've got a little something on your face," William said, laughing at his wit.

Heather ignored him and tried to stand in Ant's way, but it didn't work. "Anthurium! Stop what you're doing right this instant!" Time seemed to stand still as the room went deathly quiet. Ant stopped running, and Sweetpea ran right into him. Heather went over to Ant and scooped him into her arms. He tried licking the mud off her face, but he scowled at the awful taste. Heather laughed at his discovery, saying, "Serves you right for being such a problem child!"

After they finally got the animals to settle down, Heather and Holly wiped the mud masks from their faces. Heather checked out her shiny, glowing complexion in the mirror as she praised Holly for her horticultural genius. "This is quite something, Holly! My skin feels incredible. You should bottle this up and sell it. I bet you'd make a fortune!"

"I'm too tired right now to think about anything so complicated. I think I'm going to go say goodnight to William and head to bed. What do you think?" Holly asked.

"Great! I'll come with you and say goodnight to my little fur-child," Heather said, following Holly out into the living room. She sat next to Ant on the couch and sang him a lullaby before retiring to the bedroom with Holly. When they both looked back at William, he was lying back on the couch, Pansy still clutching to his chest. His feet hung off the edge of the couch, but he still looked as comfortable as he could, given the circumstances. Heather was much too tired to feel guilty at that moment, and she passed out within minutes once her head hit the pillow.

FIVE

Though Heather had fallen asleep right away the previous night, she only stayed asleep for a few hours. Whenever she closed her eyes, she could only see the eyes of a dead body staring back at her for help. She knew she needed some quiet time for herself to go over what had happened before she started her work for the day.

After she pulled into her parking spot on the campus, she gently picked up Ant from the passenger's seat, then headed right for the Butterfly Room. That room had charmed her since its unveiling the other day, and she knew no other place could calm her as quickly as that magical space. And she definitely needed some peace this morning.

As soon as she stepped through the doors, Ant jumped out of her arms and went chasing after the butterflies. He tried to leap as high as he could, but his little legs wouldn't carry him very far. So, he resigned himself to running around the room chaotically, growling and barking at the various colors and sizes of butterflies that floated gracefully above his head.

Heather walked over to a quiet corner and sat down on the cushioned bench, focusing solely on the smudges of color flying around the room. They appeared to her like a stunning kaleidoscope of nature that reminded her of the trips to the lake she'd taken with Marshall as a kid. As hard as she tried back then, she could never catch any of them, but it always delighted her nonetheless.

She had mourned too much death over the past several years. First, it was her brother, then Nana Moore, and then Papa Moore shortly after Nana. The fond memories she had of her childhood often felt tainted because they sometimes reminded her she could no longer wrap her arms around them or hear their contagious laughter.

Today, those memories also reminded her of something more tragic—the mystery of the dead body in Papa's potting shed. Tears fell down her cheeks as her discovery played over and over in her mind. Heather had never seen such a traumatic thing in her life, and she didn't know if she'd ever get that image out of her mind.

And even more disturbing than that, she wondered how in the world a dead body could come to be found at the new home she'd had so many fond memories of as a child. *Is this death somehow related to my family, or is it merely a coincidence that this person died on Papa's property?* With Papa gone, she felt incredibly lost as to how she should handle this situation. He had always been a kind voice of reason in her life, and now that she needed him the most, she didn't know what to do.

Ant approached Heather, wagging his tail and jumping around playfully. She called him over and hugged him tightly as he showered her with love and kisses.

"What am I supposed to do, Ant? I can't just sit around and do nothing knowing someone lost their life in our back yard."

Ant whined and nuzzled against her, as though he understood exactly what she needed.

"Is there anything I can do, little buddy?"

Heather remembered how lost she had felt upon learning

about Marshall's fatal automobile accident. It had felt like a large piece of her heart had been ripped from her when he died. Though she thought she'd feel better after the funeral, things only seemed to get worse.

That was the blessing—and the curse—of living in Washington, D.C., for as long as she did. Around every corner here at home, there were so many little reminders of the treasured family members she missed. In some moments, it felt as though she was mourning all over again, but at least now that she had reconnected with Oliver, she could begin fresh by making new memories with her family.

At that moment, Heather decided she needed to do everything she could to help get justice for the person she had found in the potting shed. As she tried to imagine how inconsolable their family members were, she knew she'd want someone in her corner if that had happened to someone she loved.

After all, that was somebody's daughter . . . somebody's son . . . somebody's everything. And they deserved the respect of Heather's effort to right whatever wrong had been done to them.

Heather stood up with Ant and took one last look at the butterflies, their beautiful colors circling the room to remind her that those who have gone before us deserve to be remembered.

Before she stepped out of the Butterfly Room, she whispered, "I *will* remember you."

When Heather got back to her office, she got Ant settled for a nap and went into the break room to grab a much-needed cup of coffee. She was having a hard time staying awake, and it would give her the kick she needed to make this workday productive.

Right when she turned around, she ran into Drusus Dudley, a world-renowned professor and expert on rubber trees who had recently become a staff member at Shellesby College.

"Oh, there you are!" Heather exclaimed, grabbing her mug of coffee. "I was just about to come looking for you."

As Professor Dudley looked for a mug to get some coffee himself, he smiled back at Heather. "Professor Moore, congratulations on the directorship. If you can do anything like the outstanding job you did at National Botanical Gardens down in Washington, D.C., I bet this greenhouse complex will become top three in the world. It's top five now, but I see even better days ahead with you at the helm."

After he got his coffee, he headed to the door and opened it for Heather. "Walk with me?"

Heather nodded at him and offered him an enthusiastic smile. "You know, I was so delighted to hear I'd be working closely with you. It's such a treat to work with the esteemed Professor Dudley!"

"Well, this job is a real step down, if I'm being honest. I was the director at Providence University, and everything was great. Then there was some stupidity with the administration, and one of the board members accused me of siphoning funds from the horticultural budget. They'd even talked a student into testifying against me. I hate that student so much. How she could testify against me is beyond me! I tutored her when she fell behind in her classes. Without my tutoring, she would have flunked out, and that was the thanks I get? Just thinking about her puts me in a rage! She ruined my career!"

Heather was completely shocked to hear this stunning admission from the professor.

"In the end, there wasn't enough evidence to prove their case, but my reputation there had been destroyed. I was blackballed in the academic community and only could get this job because I told them I'd take such a huge pay cut. I lost my home because of the legal fees I accrued during the trial and now am significantly downsized. It's so humiliating I can scarcely look other colleagues in the eye for fear of what they must think about me."

As Dudley spoke about the incident, Heather could tell he was still feeling outraged about the ordeal.

"Yikes! That is quite a story, Dudley. I'm so sorry to hear that happened to you. Though not as sorry as you'd probably want me to be, especially since it means our students will get to learn from a world-renowned horticultural expert."

"Don't get me wrong," Dudley said. "I am quite happy to be here, as it is the only paycheck I could land. But that's not the worst of that whole disaster."

What more could there be? Heather wondered. "Oh? Did something else happen?"

"I guess you could say that!" Dudley let out a derisive laugh and continued. "That student who testified against me? She had to transfer to Shellesby too! After she testified at my trial, the student body turned on her, and she started getting death threats."

"Oh, no! That's awful." *Why haven't I heard about this yet? This seems like a disaster waiting to happen!* "What's the student's name?" Heather asked.

"Mary Rose," Dudley said with a deep frown.

They had walked a complete circle in the Science Building, stopping now at Professor Dudley's office. He stood at his door and looked back at Heather.

"I have to go, I'm afraid," Dudley said, "I have a journal article I need to proof. I'm a little bit behind on my publication requirement this semester."

"Oh, sure!" Heather exclaimed. "I understand. I have a class to prepare for myself. My first one. I'm so excited!"

"Good luck, Professor!" Dudley said before he stepped into his office.

＊—❀—＊

HEATHER POPPED INTO HOLLY'S OFFICE UPON REMEMBERING HER teaching assistant had called in sick that morning, and with such a huge class, she thought she'd need the assistance. "Holly, do you mind playing substitute TA this morning? Willow has come down with something, and my class is pretty massive!"

Holly jumped up right away and grabbed her briefcase that was lying next to her desk. "Happy to help! Where is your class at?"

"I'm just on my way now." Heather looked at her watch. "We have about thirty minutes until class if you want to grab something quick from the cafeteria on the way."

"Terrific! I haven't had breakfast yet, and my blood sugar's a bit low. Let's go!" Holly walked out with Heather, and they headed down the hallway.

Once they got their food at the cafeteria, they sat down in the corner where there was a cluster of empty tables. "Are you nervous about your first class?"

"Nah. More excited than anything. I taught a lot of classes for children at the Botanical Gardens in D.C., so I'm pretty comfortable standing in front of a bunch of cranky toddlers," Heather said.

"Not much different from undergrads these days," Holly said with a laugh. "I cringe thinking about how immature I was in my freshman year!"

Heather laughed. "I wouldn't say you were immature, but you were a force to be reckoned with, that's for sure."

Holly grabbed Heather's hands and squeezed them. "I'm so glad you asked for my help! My horoscope did say I could benefit from deviating away from my normal work routine today. I think this is exactly what the doctor ordered!"

They quickly finished their food and headed to the classroom. With only five minutes to spare, most of the students were already sitting at their seats when Holly and Heather walked in. Heather flashed them a genuine smile and took her place at the podium, while Holly sat at a desk in the corner at the front of the room.

"Good morning, everyone, and welcome! My name is Professor Heather Moore, and Holly Jackson will be standing in for Willow Hanigan as my TA today. Before we get started with the lecture, Holly is going to pass out the syllabus so you can get a taste of what you'll be learning this semester."

As Holly passed out the papers, Heather took in the moment, thankful for a positive start to her teaching duties at Shellesby College. Though her personal life here wasn't starting out perfectly, she could at least focus on making the most out of her career. Heather could always count on that part of life being drama free, and she thanked her lucky stars that nothing on the landscape could change that.

SIX

Instead of grabbing lunch with Holly like she had promised her after her first class, Heather had lied and told her she had to meet with the electrician to discuss the work that had to be done on the house. She had to do something more important than gush over her glowing complexion—she had an urgent invitation to speak with Detective Huff at the station. As she sat in her car and looked up at the front door, her nerves took over, and she nearly sped away out of fear of what she might learn.

Heather let out a deep, exasperated sigh. She'd compartmentalized the fact that she had seen a dead body in her grandfather's potting shed the day before, but now, it was time to face the reality of her situation. If she ran, the detective might think she did it out of guilt. She needed to get her name as far away from the suspect list as soon as possible.

"Good afternoon, Miss Moore." Detective Huff met her at the door with a stern look on his face. He didn't seem angry; Heather figured that was probably a permanent look for him. After all, he probably had to deal with thieves and murderers all day long. He led her back to an empty interrogation room and flipped the light on. It got so bright that Heather wondered if the sun originated there. He pulled a chair out for her and took his place across the table from her.

He pulled out a folder and got right down to business. "Miss Moore, do you know a young woman by the name of Mary Rose?"

Heather was sure he said quite a bit after he mentioned the name, but she couldn't hear any of it. She had heard Mary's name uttered not even two hours ago. It was a good thing the detective wasn't paying close attention, or he would have seen her eyes open slightly in surprise. *Or maybe he did notice, and he's simply waiting for his opportunity to ask me how I killed the poor girl.*

"Hello? Miss Moore?"

The room had gone quiet, but she was too lost in her thoughts to notice. The detective let out a deep breath and repeated the tail end of his one-sided conversation. "We've identified our victim as Mary Rose, and as it turns out, she was a student at your university—Shellesby College—in your very department. Don't you think that's curious?"

Heather sat straight up and prepared to defend herself. "Well, as I've told you before, I only moved back here this week from Washington, D.C., so, likely, I never had an opportunity to meet her before she passed." *Oh, my gosh! Has she been in my potting shed all this time? This is such a disaster!*

"So, you've never met her, then?" Officer Huff asked again.

"Not in person—no. But I have to be honest . . . one of the horticulture professors at Shellesby did mention her name earlier today."

"Oh?" Detective Huff seemed interested. "And who might that be?"

"Professor Dudley. He's a—"

"Oh, good old Professor Dudley. Yes, we've learned a lot about him in the past twenty-four hours." Detective Huff flipped through his case file and pulled out a piece of paper with a bunch of scribbling on it. "Says here she testified against him in court recently. That true?"

"That's what Professor Dudley told me, but I don't know much more," Heather replied.

"Alright, then," Detective Huff said, "why don't we talk about who had access to your home before you moved in? I'm going to need a list of all the people who have been there in the past month—relatives, contractors, neighbors, and anyone else you can think of."

Heather didn't like the tone the detective was taking with her; it was almost accusatory. "Oh, sure. I'm happy to give you any information I'm privy to, Detective." She grabbed a piece of paper the detective slid across the table and started writing down all the names she could think of. The list got to be rather long because that was where they held her grandfather's wake, and some of the people in attendance she didn't even know. As she wrote, the detective watched over her shoulder.

"That's a rather long list of people. Did he run a business out of his home or something?" the detective asked.

"The wake," Heather replied softly as she continued listing names.

"So, you were there before you moved into the home?" he asked.

Heather stopped writing and looked up at Detective Huff. "Excuse me?"

"If you were at the wake, you could have very well killed Mary Rose. Isn't that right?"

"I suppose I could have killed the young woman—but I didn't." *There I go getting back on that list again.* She shook her head and handed the list to the detective now that she had finished. "Yes, of course, I attended Papa's wake because I loved him, but the truth is that I haven't made a lot of time for family the past several years. Before I moved here, I was working at the National Botanical Gardens in Washington,

D.C., and I barely even called my family let alone visited them. Ever since I graduated college, I've been very focused on my career. As a matter of fact, the last couple of times I came to Massachusetts—before I moved, I mean—was for my brother's funeral and my grandfather's funeral."

And there it was. Heather had never sat down and looked at her life that way, but it was true. She had sacrificed so much time with her family so she could build her career. By the time Marshall had died, she had to admit she didn't know a lot about his life outside of the family newsletter he had sent her every Christmas. A deep pain suddenly spread from her heart and up into her throat, making her eyes water. She didn't want to show that much of herself to the detective, so she held them back as much as she could.

Detective Huff picked up the list, then looked down at Heather. "There's one last thing I need to ask you about before you go." He slid a clear evidence bag across the table that had a custom-designed, antique ring in it. It was ornately designed with vines that seemed to snake around the circular band, all meeting up at the centerpiece of the ring—the diamond-encrusted rose at the top. "This was found on our victim's body. Does it look familiar to you?"

Heather looked up at the detective in shock. It was the very ring her grandmother had worn for decades that Heather always admired as a little girl. "It is a family heirloom that belonged to my grandmother. He bought it for her to celebrate their successful pottery business when they were younger. Through his hard work, he built that business to be a multi-million-dollar success when he sold it a few years ago. How did she get it?"

"I don't know, but I intend to find out." Detective Huff grabbed the ring from Heather and looked back at the long list of names she had given him.

After Detective Huff looked over the list, Heather stood up and approached the door. "My lunch hour is about over,

Detective. I need to head back to the campus." He didn't stop her from leaving, and she didn't look back to give him any reason to stop her.

"Oh, Miss Moore?" Detective Huff popped his head out of the room and called down the hallway to Heather. "Can you keep our conversation today confidential?" He ran to catch up to Heather so nobody would hear the rest of their conversation. "We haven't released Mary Rose's name to the public yet because her family still needs to be notified. So, I'd appreciate it if you'd keep that between you and me."

Heather hustled out of the building and back to campus. She had still had one more person to meet today. *No more drama, please*, she exhorted the universe. *I've had more than enough for this decade.*

٭ — 🐾 — ٭

HEATHER WENT INTO THE VISITOR CENTER'S KITCHEN FOR A minute to get a glass of Holly's fresh-brewed iced tea that she made each day for the greenhouse staff. She took a glass out of the cupboard and gratefully poured herself a brimming glassful. It had been a long day already at the police station, and she knew she was going to be out in the sun in a minute. She thought hydrating now would be a good idea.

I should have brought my Thermos with me. This is so good I know I'll wish to have more of this amazing tea with me on my drive this afternoon.

Right then, Poppy burst through the Visitor Center's door, loudly chewing some gum. She blew a huge bubble that popped loudly and grinned at Heather. She had on ripped jeans and a tank top that revealed a very tanned complexion. "Hi, Heather! Your chauffeur for the afternoon is ready. Your golf cart awaits." With that, Poppy did a little theatrical bow and held open the door so Heather could exit and join her in climbing in the small vehicle.

"Thanks, Poppy, I am looking forward to this drive and hearing all about this program you are running. It sounds great, and I'm glad Shellesby is a part of it."

"Oh, totally!" Poppy agreed with her and loudly smacked another two large bubbles in a row. She peeled out of the parking lot and turned right onto the dirt pathway that ringed Lake Tupelo. "The vegetable gardens are past the lake, as you know. Sit back and enjoy the ride."

They first drove alongside the little inlet that formed in this section of Lake Tupelo. The grassy banks of the lake made a type of canal in this eastern section of the body of water, and Shellesby College had created a lovely stone bridge that arched poetically above the water. Adorning the bridge was one of those lights with a hanging lantern to illuminate the way at night, those little touches of Old English architectural design being ubiquitous to the wealthy school. She strolled up onto the stone bridge and paused to admire the scenery. There was a sign posted onto one of the trees at the water's edge that read: NO FISHING, per order of Shellesby College.

"No fishing." Poppy snorted. "Would you take a look at that?" She pointed upward, and there hanging from a branch that was overhanging the water was a fishing line that had gotten stuck up there. Someone's cast had obviously been too high, and the line now was snarled around the tree branch. The blue ball of the lure hung down over the water and swung like a mobile over an infant's crib in the breeze. It provided mute testimony to the defiance of the stated prohibition of fishing there.

Heather shook her head. "Well, you know how it is. People often try to do what is expressly forbidden. It's fairly predictable if you ask me. You tell them they can't do something—they turn around and do it before a minute is out. The lake is probably filled with discarded fishing lines and lures."

"So true," Poppy said as she pulled over to the side of the dirt path to chug some fluids from the Thermos she had brought with her. "Hey, it's really hot out here today."

"Oh, it is," Heather agreed and longed again for some of that iced tea Holly had made.

She glanced down into the water and saw sunnies, which she knew were freshwater ray-finned fish native to North America. "Ah, I imagine these likely were an irresistible draw for kids during the lazy summer months when school was out," Heather said as she thought she saw a flash of a freshwater trout in the water as well.

Poppy took one last, long drink from her Thermos, tightened the cap back on, and started up the golf cart again. She and Heather made their way farther along the perimeter of Lake Tupelo. They stayed on the asphalt pathway that was about ten feet from the water's edge and soon were approaching the lawn of the college's exclusive club.

"There's the Shellesby College Club." Poppy pointed out the building.

"Oh, that must be new. I didn't see it the last year when I came for the Night Lights Gala Ball."

"Well, it's a restaurant exclusively for Shellesby alumnae, and it features a large two-story building, where they can meet, greet, and eat while enjoying live piano music inside, or you can take your cocktails outside on the terrace."

Heather turned her head to the right and could see that the restaurant was at the eastern-most edge of Shellesby College, right up next to the low stone wall that encircled the posh college.

The restaurant's guests were enjoying dinners al fresco in the delightful spring air out on the terrace. She saw that these affluent alumni had brought their dogs with them to dinner, and their children raced up and down the grassy expanse with them that led from the terrace down to the Lake Tupelo's edge. Their expensive and unusual breeds of dogs seemed exceptionally well taken care of. There was a multitude of finely brushed canines loping around and scampering on the grass with the alumnae's children.

"I would love to be able to go in there," Poppy said wistfully.

"Why can't you?" Heather asked. "You are an alumna in good standing."

"Well, currently, I'm actually sitting," Poppy laughed at her own joke and popped another couple of loud bubbles. "You may not have known my full story, but I didn't exactly leave Shellesby in good standing."

"Really? What happened to you? The last I remember, you were head of that sorority. What was it called? It was the most sought-after sorority on campus!"

"Ha! No one knows the real name anymore, but we just always called it the 'Pi Die House.'"

Heather laughed along with Poppy. "Oh yes, that's right."

"Well, it was great to be here at Shellesby and all, but I needed a little more adrenaline in my day-to-day and started shoplifting for the thrill of it. My parents are so wealthy that I certainly didn't need to do this—it was just for the adrenaline rush."

"That's a shame, Poppy. You can get a healthier and legal adrenaline rush from participating in sports. Shellesby has more sports on offer than you can shake a rake at."

"I know that, but nothing felt as awesome as getting away with it. I got away with it for four years, but then I started getting caught, and I violated my probation and stole again. So, I ended up in jail for a lengthy term."

"I'm sorry to hear that, Poppy. You were so talented and inventive, as I remember you from my classes."

"Well, you are right. I am inventive. In fact, I invented this program you are about to see today. I knew Shellesby College wasn't maximizing their vegetable garden. They only were maintaining it as a learning garden for horticulture students. I pitched the authorities in prison on the idea of running a program where inmates cultivate the garden, and the produce would be donated to the local food banks. Oh, and by the way, I would run this program as a former student of Shellesby, as I knew everything about the vegetable gardens here. They agreed to have me run it in exchange for an early release. This job is my life now!"

"Wow, that is a great idea you had! I know in these hard economic times, we must try to keep the food banks stocked. Fresh produce is always such a valuable commodity to have available for our residents."

"It is," Poppy agreed. "I think it's a win-win. The inmates gain pride in seeing their hard work in the garden pay off, and the community gains with the produce. That's why I go to any lengths to protect the program."

"Protect the program? Who would be against it?"

"Well, there was a student I denied admittance to the Pi Die sorority. Do you know how you can have a feeling about someone? You just know they aren't the right fit?" Poppy blew two more bubbles in a row that popped noisily against her cheeks.

"Well, she was definitely not the right fit for Pi Die. Too judgmental by far. So, I made the decision not to include her, and when she got wind of me running the program here, she decided to launch a vendetta against me and made it her mission to close the program down. She went to the school's paper, organized protests on campus, and even went to the *Boston Tribune*, the biggest newspaper in New England!"

"Why didn't she like it? It seems to be helping a number of people in the community out."

"She didn't have a personal feeling one way or the other— she just wanted to get back at me because I think she was quite embarrassed to have been rejected by Pi Die. I think she went through a lot of taunting and teasing because of it, but I stand by my decision. She just wasn't right for our lovely sorority."

"So, where does the program stand now?"

"Oh, let's just say I made sure that she will never again bother us. We will not have to worry about her anymore. She's done!"

"What do you mean by that?" Heather said in alarm, as this conversation seemed to take a dark turn just now. "You didn't hurt her, did you?"

"Oh, nothing like that." She chuckled a little as she began to explain how she'd gotten her revenge. "After the article came out, I thought maybe she'd like to enjoy the spoils of the program . . . quite literally. We keep a large bin of spoiled vegetables in the shed back there to make compost later. But, one day, instead of making the compost like I was supposed to, I poured all the spoiled veggies in her car with a copy of the article taped to her windshield."

"Wow. Remind me not to upset you," Heather said with a nervous laugh. It certainly wasn't as bad as she imagined, but it didn't sit quite right with Heather.

"Like I said, after that, she knows not to mess with me!" Poppy punctuated this last declaration with an extra-large bubble, popping it with barely concealed irritation. She suddenly put the golf cart back into gear and sped off.

"Hey, what's going on? This is faster than ever! How can a golf cart be going this fast?" Heather felt around frantically to hold onto the cart as it seemed to careen around corners and sharp turns in the path. Perilous with numerous exposed roots, it was a lovely pathway lined with overgrown rhododendron bushes and azaleas; however, Heather had no time to admire them as she clung on to the cart for dear life.

Poppy laughed maniacally and shouted, "Isn't this great? It's got my adrenaline going—I love it!"

"Slow down! There's a bunch of people with dogs and kids ahead! How does this go so fast, anyway?"

"My boyfriend is a mechanic. He souped it up for me with a new engine . . . and a horn!" With that, Poppy started beeping the horn incessantly as she came to a roaring halt because of the crowd blocking the pathway.

"Hey, lady! Watch out!" a mother with a twin stroller and two dogs yelled out at Poppy.

The dirt pathway had wound its way around the lake, and they came to a point that was a perfect viewing spot of the entire campus from the golf cart.

Heather was struck by the reflection of the main building in Lake Tupelo and mesmerized by the undulating surface of the water as it reflected a perfect mirror image in the lake's otherwise morning calm. The very slight breeze that blew over the lake that day constantly shifted the mirror image of the college slightly, creating a watercolor painting effect in the water. The watery image reminded her of the *Rouen Cathedral* series by Claude Monet. It became an Impressionist painting of the bucolic water scene.

Her enjoyment of the scene was suddenly broken when Poppy pocketed her phone and recklessly reversed and peeled off the dirt path and into the grassy meadow beside it. "We don't have time for this! Some of us have work to do!" Poppy blared the horn a few more times to emphasize her words.

"Your behavior is unacceptable! We welcome guests at Shellesby. Please do not be rude. You need to adhere to our code of conduct standards."

"Whatever. My boyfriend just texted me he is getting off of work early, so I want to finish up this tour and go home." Poppy headed at top speed across the meadow and zipped past a sign that read: WARNING! YOU ARE NOW LEAVING SHELLESBY COLLEGE PROPERTY. PLEASE STAY ON THE DIRT PATH AND KEEP OFF THE PRIVATE PROPERTY.

"What's going on here? This is private property!" Heather's mind was awhirl with this aggressive and unstable attitude from her former student.

"Now, I'm really feeling the adrenaline. This is awesome!" Poppy laughed as she drove quickly along the chain-link fence.

"Did you cut a hole in the fence?" Heather had seen what looked like a golf cart-sized hole in the chain-link fence, announcing the start of the private property line.

"Yup, best use of hedge clippers in a while! Settle down, Heather. I need to be able to crisscross Shellesby rapidly, and I don't have time to go slowly around the dirt path ringing the lake. These cut-throughs are so much more efficient."

"And so much more illegal too!" Heather didn't like this one bit, but now that they were zooming along inside the private property, she doubted they could exit it until they got to the far side of the fence.

Heather knew four huge estates ringed the entire southern half of Lake Tupelo. She recognized this as the Bergamore Estate, as she was treated to the sight of a fantastic Topiary Garden. This ultra-wealthy estate had built a large stone structure reminiscent of a Japanese temple upon their hillside overlooking Lake Tupelo.

"Do you think the Bergamore family will let you get away with this? They are one of the oldest and most prestigious families in the area, and they have been long-time donors and alumnae of Shellesby College. I'd be surprised if they haven't lodged several complaints about you!" It seemed as though Poppy didn't care about the consequences—she only cared about getting to their destination as fast as possible. "That is, if I don't complain about you myself!"

Finally, they tore through at lightning speed a matching door Poppy had cut out of the chain-link fence. This opening in the fence allowed them to leave the private premises and return to the dirt path along the lake. Heather saw the vegetable gardens directly ahead. *Thankfully, this reckless golf cart ride is finally over*, Heather thought as she gratefully disembarked from the vehicle, vowing not to let Poppy drive her back to the main part of campus.

"Hello, Director Moore! I'm Daphne, and I run the corrections outreach program in conjunction with Shellesby College." A pleasant woman came over to greet Heather. "As you can see, we are getting the soil prepared for the season, and we are anticipating a bumper crop of vegetables this year. Planting is underway, and the temperatures seem just right for these tiny seedlings."

Heather could see the inmates in their uniforms working on all aspects of the garden. There were women on their knees planting seedlings into the ground and placing little name placards next to the tender plants. Others were watering the soil and tilling it with hoes. She walked up to a small group planting tomatoes.

"Hi, how are you? Is this program something you would like to continue next year?" Heather asked.

The women all talked over each other with enthusiasm. Some mentioned they were inspired to try to get jobs at local nurseries now that they had hands-on experience with plants. Others said they came from the city and never had an opportunity to work with nature before. They talked of the pride they had at last year's harvest, incredulous that the little plants had grown into substantial vines of grapes, enormous zucchini, and abundant carrots and potatoes. Donating it to the food bank made them feel useful, and all agreed it was a good program for everyone involved.

"See what I mean?" Poppy had been tapping her foot with impatience, as she still seemed to be focused on leaving the campus as soon as possible to join her boyfriend on a date. "Do you see why I couldn't allow that nasty girl to interfere with this program? Well, she's out of my hair for good now!"

"So, what happened with that? Did she realize you were behind the mess in her car?" Heather asked.

"Never heard from her again. But I heard she could never get that foul smell out of car. That makes me a little happy to think about," Poppy said.

Heather was alarmed to hear this evil tone in Poppy's voice but also decided to make her move and hitch a ride back to the main campus with someone else. "Poppy, I think you can go now. I will take a little more time here, and then someone else can drive me back to campus."

Poppy looked very relieved by this and gave a curt wave and turned and vaulted into the golf cart and sped off.

Heather watched her leave just as chaotically as they had arrived together, and she felt grateful she wouldn't have to endure a golf cart ride like that ever again. To calm herself down, she enjoyed talking to the women working on the plants and chatted with them pleasantly, noticing they took great pride in the work they were doing.

When she was ready to leave, Heather said her goodbyes to the women and the director, then cautiously stepped into a waiting golf cart to head back to campus. Her white-knuckle grip on the dashboard relaxed as soon as she realized the new driver escorting her back to the campus was a much better driver than Poppy.

As they arrived back at the main building, all Heather could think about was driving to William's Cot' so she could take a shower and head to bed after this very long and draining day. *No more golf cart rides for me, thank you very much!* she thought to herself as she stepped into her vehicle and headed for her temporary home.

SEVEN

When the weekend came around, Heather focused her attention on learning more about Mary Rose and how she might have met her end in her grandfather's potting shed. Upon waking that Saturday morning, she saw Pansy sleeping comfortably in William's lap and looked back at Holly, who had just showered and gotten dressed. "Do you think it would be okay if I left Pansy with you and William for a couple of hours? The electrician is working over at the house, and I wanted to stop by and check on the progress."

"You're totally fine! I think I'm going to let William and his new bestie sleep for a while. Do you want some company? I don't have much planned for the day," Holly said.

Heather grabbed Ant's leash and shook it until Ant came running. "No, I'll be fine. Besides, I've got my trusty sidekick here to keep me out of trouble!" She hoped Holly would leave it at that because she wasn't sure she was ready to explain the real reason she wanted to stop by her house.

Holly smiled. "No worries. I'll be around if you change your mind and want to have lunch out or something. I think I could use some time away from the Cot' myself today."

With that, Heather left with Ant quickly before Holly had time to wake up more and insist that she come with her. As soon as they got into Heather's car, she sped out of the driveway, heading down the road. "That was a close one, buddy! I thought for sure she might not take no for answer. We've got to keep this a secret between you and me for now. The less they know about Mary Rose, the better."

As she turned into her neighborhood, her guilt started creeping up on her. "I know we probably shouldn't be back here, but I need some answers. I can't stand the thought of our family name being tarnished by this poor girl's murder. I know *I* didn't do it, but who did? Maybe there's something the detective missed lying around in the potting shed."

When Heather pulled onto her dead-end street, she saw a familiar vehicle parked dangerously close to her driveway. It was the delivery van for Thornton's Flower Company she had seen driving around town so many times before. "That's strange. What in the world are they doing at my house?" As she slowed down, she looked high and low for any sign of Sunny's delivery driver, but she couldn't see anyone out on the street delivering flowers.

Strange. Why would they be out here if they're not delivering flowers? Heather turned that thought over and over in her mind, but she couldn't make sense of it. She knew, though, that if she didn't leave the area immediately, she'd risk running into whoever was driving the delivery van. So, she took off with no real destination in mind.

"What do you make of that, Ant? Must be a coincidence." Her partner in crime didn't have much to say in response, so Heather let her head keep spinning around and around about the mysterious delivery van sitting in front of her house. Then, when she finally remembered what she had found in the shed before calling the police, she freaked out.

"No, no, no, no, no! It can't be! Do you think Sunny's delivery driver had something going on with Mary, and he's returning to get rid of the evidence now that they've found her body?" The more Heather let that thought dance around in her mind, it didn't seem too outrageous.

Ant cocked his head at Heather as if he had something to say about it.

"Well, it's not any crazier than finding a dead body in Papa's shed!"

Before she knew it, she found herself only a few blocks away from Thornton Flower Company, and she had to see what all this business was all about. When she pulled into their parking lot, she saw the offending van sitting right there in front of her. "Of course, they could have more than one. Why didn't I write down the plate number? That wasn't very smart of Mommy, was it?" She turned to Ant and picked him up before getting out of the car.

The bell on the door rang as Heather walked through, but she didn't see anyone inside. "Hello? Is anybody home?" She stepped up to the counter when nobody responded and rang the bell for service like the sign instructed.

"Just a minute! I'm on my way!" Sunny called from around the corner.

"Oh, it's just you." Sunny put the orchids on the counter and took her place of dominance next to the cash register. "Why have you brought that mutt into my flower shop?" She frowned at Heather as she looked her up and down.

"Gee, I hope you don't greet all your customers like that," Heather said with a laugh. "And by the way, I'll have you know he's not a mutt—he comes from a long line of Westminster Kennel Club Champions!"

"Is that what you are? A customer?"

Normally, Heather would be downright mad about somebody insulting her precious baby like that, but this was Sunny Thornton. She was not known for her friendly demeanor. In fact, there wasn't one person in town Sunny acted like she could halfway tolerate. Why she wanted to run a flower shop was a mystery to Heather, but she was still a great floral designer. "Well, no, I guess not." She placed Ant gently down on the counter directly in front of Sunny, and she backed away like he was a bomb about to explode in her face. "I saw your delivery van in front of my house, and I—"

Sunny shook her head. "No, you must be mistaken."

"No, ma'am, I am not mistaken because I saw it with my own two eyes." Heather raised her voice and put her hands on her hips.

"Are you calling me a liar?" Sunny asked.

"I said nothing of the sort! I only came to ask if there had been any deliveries on Stonelily Drive—that's all." Heather relaxed a little bit now that she had gotten her question out in the open.

"Oh, no." Sunny's voice got low. "Not that I know of, but I'll check the computer just to be sure." She carefully walked toward her computer, trying her hardest not to get close to Ant. After typing for a few seconds, she looked back at Heather. "Nothing in the computer either." Sunny walked around to the display closest to Heather and said, "I was surprised to see you at the flower market the other day."

"Well, I just had to get my hands on a bunch of those rainbow lilies. They were stunning, weren't they?" Heather walked around the shop, browsing through all the merchandise Sunny had for sale.

Sunny shrugged. "I suppose they were alright. You know, I heard some crazy florist deliberately set off the alarm so he could steal some of those lilies."

"No! Seriously? Well, it figures. You'd think the flower and plant industry would be calm, cool, and collected, but it's quite the opposite, isn't it?" Heather asked.

Sunny laughed. "It certainly can be!"

Heather stopped suddenly and looked all around the shop. "Wow, that chocolate smell from the bakery across the street is pretty strong! How do you work here all day and not gain 100 pounds? I'd be over there several times a day!"

"Oh, dear, that's not chocolate you're smelling. It's a shipment of chocolate cosmos we got in just today. Stay here just a minute, and I'll bring some out to show you." Sunny was only gone for a minute, then came right back into the front of the flower shop carrying a large crate full of burgundy-colored flowers that had a slight resemblance to a daisy except for having larger petals.

"I think this is what you're smelling." Sunny brought the crate closer to Heather to let her smell their resemblance to hot chocolate.

"These are absolutely intoxicating. What a treat!" Heather exclaimed as she made a mental note to talk to William about getting a chocolate cosmos exhibit set up at Shellesby. She picked Ant off the counter and showed him the flowers. "Check out these pretty flowers, Ant! Aren't they amazing?"

Sunny shook her head and laughed. "I know—they're one of my favorites. It's the first time we've gotten them in since the disaster last year. I just couldn't bring myself to purchase them again for such a long time." She set them down on the counter and turned back to Heather.

"Oh, goodness! It sounds like you have a story indeed. What happened last year? I didn't hear about this!"

"I'm surprised you didn't hear about it from your grandfather when it happened," Sunny said.

"My grandfather? What does he have to do with it?" Heather asked.

"Well, we had a wholesale account with him for many years. We were getting ready for one of our biggest events and placed a pretty big order for some unique pots his designer custom-made just for our company that featured our logo. They were delivered a few days before our event. They looked stunning, and some of our customers even purchased several of them. As a matter of fact, it was the one day in the history of our company that we made the most sales." The phone rang, interrupting their conversation. Sunny returned a few minutes later to continue.

"I don't get it," Heather said. "If it was so successful, then how was it a disaster?"

"Well, that came after. Within two weeks of the event, we had so many angry calls from our customers about the pots we sold at the event. Every single plant they tried to grow in the pots died—they couldn't get anything to grow in them! So, I did the only thing I could do . . . I refunded their money. All told, that was a six-figure loss for the shop, and it nearly destroyed us."

"Wow! I'm so sorry to hear that. How long did it take to get a refund from my grandfather?" Heather asked.

"That's just it," Sunny said with a hint of anger in her voice. "He never did. He wouldn't even give me money or even any credit for future orders. So, we were stuck with all these bad pots we couldn't do anything with."

"That doesn't sound right to me," Heather said. "I've never known Papa to make bad business decisions like that. I feel quite sure he would have refunded your money."

Sunny shook her head. "I don't know what to tell you. He sent someone over to personally tell me that he had no plans of returning the money. You can bet I called him straight away to give him an earful about that!"

"And what did he say?" Heather asked.

"Well, he changed his tune, didn't he? He got caught trying to hurt my business and said he planned to fix the oversight right away. Of course, that never happened. I think he just said that to buy some time . . . because, to this day, I've never been paid back for all that mess."

After that, Heather was no longer in the mood to talk about all this disaster, so she said her goodbyes and headed back out to her car with Ant. She had a really hard time believing the entire story Sunny had told her. Heather had never known her grandfather to be unreasonable—not in his personal life and certainly not in his professional life. She'd love to know what really happened, but it didn't seem like there was anyone around who could confirm or deny Sunny's story. So, she tried to put it out of her mind.

As a distraction, she took out her cell phone to scroll through Instagram for some plant inspiration for some upcoming projects at work, and the first picture that popped up hit her like train wreck. It was a selfie of Oliver and his ex-girlfriend kissing each other. The caption read: *We may not have had the perfect relationship, but you were the love of my life, Mary Rose. #truelove #loveofmylife #restinpeace #imissyoualready #loveyouforever.*

Mary Rose. Oliver's ex-girlfriend was Mary Rose. How had that slipped by Heather? Now, so many things made so much more sense. She wrestled with her mind about whether she should go to Detective Huff with this new realization or not. If he found out she had known, he would certainly be a lot more suspicious of her for hiding the information. But if she told him right now, she felt like maybe she'd be admitting Oliver had killed Mary without giving him a chance to tell his side of the story.

She turned to Ant with tears in her eyes. "I've got to get in that shed . . . tonight!"

——🐾——

WHEN HEATHER WALKED BACK INTO THE COT', HOLLY WAS throwing some cut vegetables into a pot to make some stew for her and William's lunches for the upcoming week. Heather looked around the living room, but William was nowhere to be found. She wasn't sure she could handle breaking into a crime scene all on her own, and she planned to recruit Holly.

"Psst! Holly!" Heather tried to be as quiet as she could in case William was still in the apartment. "Do you want to go on an adventure?"

Holly looked up with excitement in her eyes, and she dropped the spoon she held in her hand. "Oh my gosh, yes! What's going on?"

Heather nodded her head toward the front door and stepped outside to wait for Holly. "I've been lying to you about my house."

"Why? What happened?"

"I'll tell you, but you have to promise to keep it a secret from William. Can you do that?" Heather asked.

Holly looked over at their bedroom window, then back at Heather. "I don't like keeping secrets from William. Why can't we tell him?"

"We can—just not yet. I just need to keep my involvement with this matter quiet for a little bit longer. Do you think you can help with that?"

Holly let out a deep sigh. "Ok, but this is a one-time deal. Now, tell me . . . what's going on?"

Before Heather could answer Holly, William stepped outside with Pansy in his arms. Right as he was about to say something, Pansy let out a loud, drawn-out *meow*, and William nearly had a fit.

"Oh my god, Holly, did you hear that? She just said I love you!"

Holly rolled her eyes and pointed toward the door. "If you go in the house right now, I will forget you ever said that." Holly glared at William, and he walked away, sulking inside, with Pansy in tow.

"You see what I have to deal with?" Holly laughed. But when she looked over at Heather, she had tears falling down her face. "Oh, no! What is it? What's wrong?"

"Do you trust me, Holly?" Heather said, wiping the tears from her face.

"Only with my life!" Holly exclaimed.

"You're going to think this is a joke, but it's really not." Heather stopped to gather the courage to continue. "But I found something in the shed at the house. I've been lying to you about the electricity."

"Heather? What's going on? What could be so bad that you have to lie about it?" Holly asked.

"I found a dead body. There was a dead body in my potting shed."

Holly shook her head and stepped back a bit. "Wait a minute. You're serious? You found a dead body?"

Heather looked toward the house to make sure William wasn't nearby. She looked inside the window and saw him chatting away with Pansy while Ant watched them, wagging his cute little tail. "Can we have this conversation on the way to the house? I'd like to get over there and check a few things out."

Holly popped inside to say goodbye to William, then they both jumped in the car and took off toward Stonelily Drive.

"Haven't you heard the news going around at Shellesby? She was a student . . . in *our* department! And to think . . . she was lying there dead in my shed on that first day I moved in. It's given me the creeps just thinking about it."

"What was her name?" Holly asked.

Heather pulled into her driveway, then pressed the button to open the automatic garage door. "Mary Rose." She turned off the car as quickly as she could and shut the garage door so nobody could see that they were there. Heather waited for her friend to step out of the vehicle, but she just sat there, looking like she was in shock. She opened the door and helped Holly out of the car.

Holly looked up at Heather, and her face looked as white as a ghost. "I know her. She's dead? I know her."

Heather led Holly into the kitchen and sat her down at the table. She made a glass of ice water and sat it in front of her. "I think you *are* in shock. Drink some water—it will make you feel better."

"Thank you. I just need a minute." Holly sat there, drinking her water, then she sat it down on the table, her face suddenly frozen.

"Holly, what is it? What's wrong?"

"This is a crime scene, Heather. You've brought me to an active crime scene? We're not supposed to be here, are we?" Holly asked.

Heather wondered if it was a bad idea to bring Holly into the fold. She knew Holly was no stranger to crazy things happening in her life, but she also didn't consider that she might have been close to Mary Rose. "Look, Holly, I'm sorry I brought you into this. Maybe I should just take you back home. I feel bad now for dragging you into my mess."

Holly stood up and gave Heather a big hug. "Don't you dare do that! You need help, and I'm here to help you. What are best friends for if not to help them break into a crime scene at their own house?"

Heather laughed and felt around in her purse, then pulled out some surgical gloves. "Well, we'll probably need these— you know, just in case the police come back. Wouldn't want them to find your fingerprints all over the shed!"

Before Holly put her gloves on, she grabbed onto Heather's arm. "Can I ask you one question before I agree to all this?"

Heather nodded her head.

"Why are you getting involved with this? Shouldn't it be the police's job to look for clues?"

"I can't stop thinking about Mary, about how she died. Someone just killed her and left her there to rot. I have nightmares. I can't sleep. I can't stop thinking about her lying there helpless. I feel like I have a responsibility to do everything I can so her family can get justice."

Holly pulled on her gloves and stood up. "Detective Heather Moore. I kind of like how that sounds." She offered Heather a smile, and they both walked out into the back yard.

When they got inside the shed, Heather thought she smelled a faint chocolate scent again. "Do you smell that? What does that remind you of?"

Holly looked around the shed, then back at Heather. "Heather, have you been holding out on me? A murder shed *and* a secret stash of chocolate bars? You are a dangerous person to know! Where did you hide the chocolate?"

"I've already looked. As a matter of fact, that's how I found the . . . the . . . body." Heather pointed to the cupboard that was still wide open. "That's where they found her, where they found Mary."

"What do you suppose she was doing here in the shed, anyway?" Holly asked.

"Well, she worked for Papa for a little bit. She designed the pottery they made on commission and helped streamline that process," Heather said. "But it is curious that she'd show up here after his death. What could she have been looking for?" Heather said that last line more to herself than Holly. It definitely seemed strange that an ex-employee would show up after her employer died. "Besides, I heard he fired her, so it seems a bit suspicious that she'd show back up to the estate."

They both stepped back and stared at the open cabinet drawer. Holly crept closer to it and peeked inside, but it was empty now. She turned back to Heather. "Her body was in here?"

Holly got closer and felt around the cabinet to see if the police had left anything behind. "I think I found something!" She pulled out a thick envelope, and when she opened it, they both stood in a state of shock.

Heather backed away from the envelope upon seeing a

thick stack of one-hundred dollar bills. "That's a lot of money. Papa was very smart about his money . . . knew exactly what was in his account at any given moment. He wasn't the type of person who would leave it lying around like that."

"Maybe I'll just put this back in there . . . for now . . . until we know why it's here." But, when she came back out, she had a flower in her hand. "Do you know what kind of flower this is?" Lowering her head close to the flower, Holly sniffed it. "Oh, my goodness! This is the chocolate smell I've been smelling."

"No! Put that back in there! We shouldn't be messing with anything here," Heather said, then focused back on the flowers. They no longer had their chocolatey velvet color, but Heather knew exactly what kind of flowers they were because she had seen them at Sunny's shop earlier that day.

Holly placed the flowers back where she found them, then let out a deep sigh. "I guess that means there's no *real* chocolate here."

"Those . . . are . . . chocolate cosmos." Heather stepped closer to the dead flowers and took a picture with her cell phone. She didn't want to mess with anything at the crime scene because she knew it was possible Detective Huff would be back to look for any clues he had missed.

Holly asked, "Do you think the murderer left these flowers?"

Heather backed away from the cabinet. "No, they couldn't be. There is absolutely no way." *After all, what reason would Sunny Thornton have for killing a young botany student? It simply doesn't make sense.* "Papa probably left them there. Given the state of the garden in his old age, it wouldn't surprise me if he had a bunch of dead flowers laying around here." The more she thought about it, the more Heather thought it was merely a distraction. "Besides, they're not poisonous as far as I know. How would they have killed Mary with them?"

Holly started laughing uncontrollably as she stepped

away from the cabinet. "Heather, can you imagine? Something that smells like chocolate being poisonous? That seems like it should be illegal. Chocolate lovers everywhere would revolt!"

Heather had to admit it was pretty funny, and she laughed right along with Holly.

"You have to admit, though, it wouldn't be a bad way to go—that is, if they actually tasted like chocolate too!" Holly said.

"I'd overdose in a heartbeat!"

"Same!"

After they stopped laughing and suddenly remembered a dead body had been in the shed not long ago, Heather took one last look around the shed. "It seems like the police have pretty much cleaned up the entire scene. There are not many clues here to go on."

They both agreed it was best if they headed back to the Cot' right away before the police caught wind of their presence at the crime scene. On the way home, Heather called Sunny Thornton to ask her about the chocolate cosmos.

"I'm sorry, Heather, but I've just sold my last bunch of them. They don't last long around here this close to Mother's Day. But the vendor I got these from is going to be at the Boston Flower Market tomorrow morning. And if you plan on going, I wouldn't get there any later than five. You know how those crowds can be!"

When they got back to the Cot', William had tons of questions about what they had been up to, but neither of the women said much of anything. Holly simply planted a passionate kiss on his lips and said with a wink, "It's a surprise! You'll find out soon enough."

After dinner, Heather excused herself and went into Holly and William's bedroom to write an email to Lars in private right before heading to bed. It had been a long day, and she figured tomorrow would be another long and stressful day if her trip to the Cambridge Flower Market was any indication of what was to come in Boston.

TO: Lars Oslo
FROM: Heather Moore
SUBJECT: Boston Flower Market

Well, I guess I'm going to head out to the Boston Flower Market in the morning. I've just learned about these delightful flowers called "chocolate cosmos" that smell heavenly and are about as beautiful as they smell! Being obsessed with chocolate as I am, I can't pass up a chance to get my hands on those babies.

What about you? What are you up to this weekend?

My first week at my new job has been rather interesting! I've met some colorful characters, that's for sure, and I'm sure next week will be just as interesting. I guess I'd forgotten how intense it can be surrounded by so many people in the plant and flower world! There's certainly some craziness that's bound to happen . . . and it seems like it's stalking me around every corner.

Anyway, I'll sign off for now. I have to get up early if I'm going to make it to Boston by five. I can't wait to hear from you again!

EIGHT

Heather stood in front of the dark window that looked out into Holly and William's garden. Like she had expected, their backyard looked like a proper botanical garden with rose bushes in an array of colors that created the foundation for a miniature maze with their zig-zag patterns. And from where she stood, she saw a beautiful, tinted floodlight that highlighted the treasure the maze led to—a proper herb and vegetable garden that had everything a gourmet cook would ever need. Heather had a chance to taste a variety of food Holly had made over the years from their vegetable garden, and they had to be the best-tasting veggies she ever had in her life.

The coffee pot stopped brewing, and she poured herself a huge cup to take on the road with her to the Boston Flower Market. She made herself and Ant a quick breakfast, then gathered her things to head out the door. On her way to the front door, Holly stepped out of the bedroom, yawning and squinting at Heather. "Headed to the market?" she mumbled.

"Yes, it's about that time. Want to come with me?" Heather asked.

Holly glared at Heather and let out a derisive laugh.

"Sorry, but I am adamantly against mornings. You and Ant are on your own."

Heather smiled and walked outside with Ant trailing not far behind her. When they got into the car, Ant passed out right away, leaving Heather to keep herself company all on her own. Unlike their last trip to a flower market, she had watched the forecast so she could plan accordingly. "No April showers today, buddy!" She hoped that was a good sign because she didn't want to relive the events of the last flower market they had attended.

When they pulled into the parking lot, it almost looked as packed as it had when they went to the Cambridge Flower Market, but she had a much easier time finding a parking spot today. "Wow! It *has* been a long time since I've been here, Ant! Everything looks so different that I almost don't recognize a thing. They must have done a lot of remodeling over the years."

Ant looked up at Heather and cocked his head, then started sniffing around on the ground.

"Oh, no! We don't have time for potty right now. If you hang on until we find those special flowers, then we'll find a nice patch of grass for you to relieve yourself." Heather started speed walking through the entrance of the market, pulling Ant behind her.

"Aha! Ant, if my instincts are correct, the vendor should be just about three stalls ahead of us!"

Heather confidently poked her head around the beginning of row A, having traversed the entire length of aisle two, and honing in on where she thought the specific vendor was located, per Sunny's instructions.

Right then, Ant had enough of waiting for Heather. His bladder emergency got much more imminent, and he barreled toward a flower display at top speed. He headed to the lowest flowers without stopping, right next to the floor.

He lifted up his leg when she heard the vendor start to screech.

"Hey! You break—you buy!"

Heather laughed. "Well, I don't think he actually broke anything, but I will give you money for that bunch of flowers anyway." She saw a sign that proclaimed them to be $3.00, so she pulled out a $5.00 bill and pressed it into the irate vendor's hand.

"Keep the change," she whispered as Ant finished and happily trotted off again in search of new adventures.

"There it is, Ant! One stall down! Let's go, boy!" Heather's eyes spied the lone bunch of chocolate cosmos in a display only ten feet ahead of her. Jogging these last few steps, she loudly exclaimed, "Eureka, I got it!" only to have her happiness instantly dashed as another hand closed over hers and started to try to take it out of her grasp.

"Hey, hey! What's going on here?" She looked incredulously up and into the grinning face of Lars Oslo. Trying to dislodge his hand proved futile as he had a death grip on these rare flowers.

"Heather, good morning! Fancy seeing you here today." Lars smiled at Heather, yet he never quite let go of the flowers. He was a man on a very important mission that morning.

"Well, it is neither a good morning with you trying to steal my bunch of flowers nor a surprise that I would be here, as I emailed you as much last night." Heather tried to pull the flowers gently away from him, but it was no use. She could have gotten them away from him with a little more force, but then the flowers would be ruined.

"And so you did and thank you for that because the ambassador to Norway is coming through Boston on his way back to Europe. My family has connections to him, and I was going to host a dinner party for him at my house. His wife is a chocoholic, and I wanted to impress them both with these flowers." His smile still didn't drop, but Heather didn't think his expression matched his actions. She was starting to rethink her attraction toward him now if this was what he was willing to do for something he wanted.

"That is all well and good, Lars, but I saw these first, and I need them for a project, so if you'll just unhand them, please, we can all be happy." Heather tried to push his body away, but he was much too strong for her. There was no winning against him—she'd need to convince him to give up if she wanted to walk away with the chocolate cosmos.

Ant started to pick up on Heather's irritation and decided to jump in to protect her. He growled in his cute way, hardly scaring anyone with that tiny, high-pitched growl, but what he lacked in fearsomeness, he made up with enthusiasm, barking up a storm. Passersby started to take notice, watching as the tiny thing did as much damage as he could with his miniature frame.

Lars raised his voice to be heard over Ant's frenetic barking. "Heather, my dear, I would love to let you have these, too, like with the rainbow lilies, but I do need to impress the ambassador and his wife. They are loyal donors to Middleton, and we rely on their generous monetary gifts to keep our greenhouse running."

Heather felt a pang of regret, as she knew how important donor dollars were for an institution, but she needed to see if these flowers matched the dead ones in her potting shed, and she had a mystery to solve. She strengthened her resolve and steeled her heart against the plea in his warm brown eyes, insisting he allow her to have them.

Ant now deployed his one and only nuclear option and started gnawing on his pants leg, shaking his head back and forth fiercely with a mouthful of his clothing.

"Anthurium! Mind your manners! Let go of Lars' pants leg at once!"

Ant blithely ignored the admonishment and redoubled his

efforts in chewing through the clothes to get at Lars' Achilles tendon.

"I will have to concede defeat, dear Heather. The chocolate cosmos bunch is yours! I don't want to aggravate the little guy any further than I already have. I will have to make do with some roses for the dinner with the ambassador." Lars held up his hands dramatically and reached for a few bunches of roses.

"It's alright, Ant. He gave us the flowers. You can calm down now." She gently stroked his head as Ant gave a few more half-hearted growls in Lars' direction, then relaxed in her arms.

"Here, let me pay for these precious flowers that caused such a ruckus this morning. One of these days, Ant, I look forward to attending a flower market without all the drama." Heather smiled as she maneuvered Ant around in her arms so she could dig out a bill to pay the vendor for her bunch.

"Well, if we are all friends again, how about some breakfast?" Lars asked. "I know the best little eatery right around the block. It's called Pancake Paradise, and you can choose any style of pancake and any flavor syrup and topping—and they have tons to choose from."

"Pancake Paradise does sound amazing, but I have Ant. I doubt they'll let us in with him."

Ant looked back and forth between Heather and Lars as they engaged in conversation. He was ready, willing, and able to carry out his duty as protector should the perpetrator get out of hand. Nobody would hurt Heather under his watch!

"Let's go see, and I'll try to work my magic on the staff and smuggle him in somehow."

Heather smiled at him. "Ok, that sounds like a plan!"

They walked briskly out of the market, and he led her down one of the narrow streets in Boston's downtown financial district. The flower market and Boston Botanical Gardens were located in this eastern part of the city, close to the wharves where boats and ships came daily with goods from around the world. He took her hand, because suddenly, the part of the sidewalk they were walking on was broken up and sealed off as it was under construction, so he veered them into the street for a few yards to pass that obstacle. When they re-emerged and could get back on the sidewalk, she noticed he didn't let go of her hand . . . *And it felt pretty good!*

"Have you been to Pancake Paradise before?" Heather asked.

"Oh yes, my job sees me showing up at the flower market from time to time, and I discovered this little out-of-the-way place when I walked back to my car one day. I caution you, though. The food is so good and the seating so limited we might have to wait awhile."

"How long is awhile?" Heather looked down at his strong hand still holding onto hers. She blushed a little and hoped with all her might it would stay attached to hers for just a little bit longer.

"Oh, if we're lucky, maybe two hours." His voice got a little quiet toward the end.

"*TWO HOURS!* Surely, you are joking." Heather stopped walking mid-step but still hung on firmly to Lars' hand. She'd never heard of such a thing! *A pancake place with a two-hour wait? Are they made out of solid gold? He's got to be joking!*

"Certainly not. They only have five indoor tables."

"If they're so popular, why don't they expand to a larger space?" Heather started walking again, letting Lars lead the way.

"I don't know. You'll have to ask the owner yourself. All I know is that they have the best pancakes I've ever eaten."

"Well, now I'm as curious as can be. I can't wait to see this place and their food!"

"You won't have to wait long. Look, there it is!"

Heather followed his free hand and saw him point to a rather nondescript small restaurant with a huge banner proclaiming, "'The Best Pancakes Winner' Boston Dining Magazine 2022" over the door. And what a door! A line stretched around the block, twice over. It was a double-rowed line with people patiently chatting or consulting their phones, presumably settled in for the duration.

Heather squeezed his hand warmly. "You weren't kidding, were you?"

"Not at all. Here, come with me. I am about to work a little Lars magic on the staff." He led her to the host stand placed outside to register parties for the waiting list. "Excuse me, is Laura on duty today?"

The hostess smiled and said, "Yes, she is. May I tell her who is asking for her?"

"Please tell her I'm Lars from Middleton. She'll recognize my name."

"Will do, sir. Wait right here."

"Laura?" Heather asked with an arched eyebrow.

"She's the owner. I happened to come in on the day her beloved cat passed away, and she was a wreck. I told her my sister just had kittens, and while her cat isn't the same breed she had, I showed her a picture on my phone, and she instantly fell in love. Nothing can replace her beloved Daisy, naturally, but the promise of a new kitten seemed to be the only way to heal the hole in her heart. She always gets me in for a table quickly ever since."

"That's a beautiful story. You have a good heart."

Right then, a perky woman bounded through the door, and when she caught sight of Lars, her face lit up in a huge smile. "Lars! What a surprise. You should have called me earlier so I could save your favorite table. As it is, it might be a ten-minute wait or so. That party just doesn't want to leave and even ordered one more short stack right now for takeout!"

"Who can blame them, Laura? You have the best pancakes this side of paradise."

Laura grinned at the joke.

"Listen, Laura, can you step away with us a few feet? I have something to ask you without all the crowd listening in."

"Sure, Lars, let's go around to the back door for a second." Laura led them around back to where the al fresco dining tables were.

"Laura, meet Heather, my new friend."

"How are you doing, Heather? That is sure a beautiful bunch of flowers! I see a lot of customers with flowers since we are so close to the market, but I don't think I ever saw that species before."

"Hi Laura, it's great to meet you! I doubt you have seen these before. This is nearly the first time I saw them myself. They are called chocolate cosmos. Have you noticed the chocolatey smell?" Heather pushed the flowers toward Laura.

"I smell our chocolate toppings all day—I might as well be working in a candy store! I didn't realize the current smell is from your flowers." With that, Laura leaned in for a good whiff of the bunch Heather held.

"My word! They do smell like chocolate. What amazing flowers they are."

"Laura, can you please consider doing us a big favor? May we sit al fresco out here, as Heather has her little dog, Ant, with her today." When Ant growled up at Lars, he took a step away from him just to keep the peace.

"That is a great idea, Lars! We aren't opening up al fresco tables today because there is that huge cloud hanging over us, and I feel a drop of rain from time to time. April showers and all! But for you, of course, we will do it." Laura led them over to a table that sat underneath a large umbrella. "At least this cover will give you a little bit of protection if it decides to rain again."

"Yes, we see the cloud, too, but we would be thrilled to start here, and if the downpours come, we will quickly box it up for takeout and get back to our car." Lars pulled out a chair for Heather and made sure she got situated comfortably.

"That is a sweet deal, and I will also come back with a bowl of water for Ant and a bucket to put those flowers in. Can't have them outside of water for too long. They look too precious to allow to wilt. Let me quickly grab you two menus, and I'll be back with the rest." Laura left for a few minutes, giving them both some time to revel in their victory.

"What did I tell you?" Lars asked as he pulled up a chair next to Heather and brushed up against her leg. "Laura is simply the best restaurant owner there is in Boston. She can't be beaten!" He beamed at Heather and gazed longingly into her beautiful eyes.

Heather jumped slightly, interrupting the romantic trance Lars had put on her, when Laura returned with two menus in her hand. She didn't want to be rude at all—and was certainly grateful for Laura's hospitality—but she kept thinking how she'd rather be alone with Lars. The more time she spent with him, the more time she wanted the entire world to disappear. She'd forgotten entirely about the perceived rudeness of the chocolate cosmo debacle and couldn't imagine this gorgeous man in front of her had an unkind bone in his body.

"You're the best! How is Bluebell?"

"She's the best kitten I ever had. The sweetest little snuggler you ever saw. I can't thank you enough, Lars, and your sister." Laura pulled out her cell phone to show both Heather and Lars her pride and joy, a British shorthair with a blue-gray coat aptly named Bluebell.

"I'll be sure to tell her. What great news! And I can't believe how big Bluebell has gotten. Do you mind sending me a couple of these photos? Iris would love to see how happy she is with you and your family."

Heather peeked around the corner and saw that the line to get inside had gotten even longer. "Boy, did you work a miracle here! That wait up there is two hours at least—probably even longer now."

"I did tell you so, and once you taste the pancakes, you will see why. Thank you, Laura." Lars smiled his gratitude as Laura placed the two menus on the table and hustled toward the back door, disappearing into the kitchen.

Lars grabbed the menus and slid one over to Heather. As he explained everything, he pointed to various parts of the menu. "So, the way this works is you choose your pancake type, your syrup, and your topping. Mix and match all the way. Or you can choose the dishes on the right side of the menu." His finger slid down the long list of gourmet pancakes that were unique to Pancake Paradise.

Heather's eyes gleamed as she took in the beautiful menu, replete with large glossy photos of some of the pancake and topping combinations. "Hawaiian hotcakes with coconut syrup and pineapple topping. Georgia griddlecakes with peach syrup and whipped crème. Sin City silver dollars with chocolate syrup and mint topping. Oh my goodness, how am I ever to choose, Lars?"

"That is indeed the million-dollar question today! Oh, have you seen . . . it's at the bottom . . . Boston Johnnycakes, one syrup if by land and two toppings if by sea...do you remember that famous line 'one if by land and two if by sea' signal from the Revolutionary War?"

"How could I forget? Ohhh, check this out—my favorite!" Heather read excitedly from the list on the right. "The Maine Event. Buckwheat pancakes with maple syrup and a side of Maine lobster meat."

"Don't forget to look at all the other ala carte mix and match ones before you settle on that one, though you might have a hard time beating the Maine Event."

She scanned the left side of the menu and saw an eye-popping assortment of options. Savoring each word under her breath, she read quietly, "Whole wheat pancakes, oatmeal pancakes, rice-flour pancakes, gluten-free pancakes, bran pancakes, brown rice-flour pancakes, almond-flour pancakes, spelt pancakes, and cornmeal-flour pancakes! My brain cannot take all those options in, Lars. I need to come here every day for a month. How can I be expected to just choose one on demand right now?" Heather laughed heartily.

"Yes, yes, I feel your pain and will now turn the screws on you even further. Let's review the syrup choices: strawberry, marshmallow, peach, chocolate, maple, pineapple, blueberry, and caramel," Lars said with a wicked gleam in his eye.

"Stop! I don't even want to review the toppings because I know I can't make it out here every day, and the more I read, the more I will want to just rent an apartment across the street from this restaurant and be done with it."

"Well, what do you think about a breakfast here every Sunday?" Lars smiled warmly at her, and Heather snapped her head up from perusing the menu and felt butterflies zoom around in her belly. A stray sunbeam peeked from behind the big cloud above and highlighted his hair, giving it a most attractive shine. His eyes twinkled as he took in her obvious enjoyment of the menu options. She was about to respond when Laura came back with a dish of water for Ant and a nice bucket filled with water for her chocolate cosmos flowers.

She also placed a basket that was lined with a checkered cloth and full of fresh-baked goods, including small corn muffins, biscuits, and rolls with pats of butter and little jars of jam on the table. "Have you decided on your order, friends?"

"Heather, dear, you are catching flies, I am afraid," Lars said. "I understand completely. I felt like this myself my first few times here. It is called Pancake Paradise, after all."

"This is indeed a most delightful restaurant, and I hardly can decide, so I think I will go with the Maine Event and the Hawaiian Hotcakes and eat one from each and take the rest home."

"Perfect choice. I'll have the cornmeal pancakes, Laura, with caramel syrup and toasted almond topping, please."

With the ordering finished, both peered under the table to see Ant enjoying a nice drink from his bowl of water. Afterward, he stretched out at her feet, and she bent down to stroke his head to comfort him.

"How is your Achilles, by the way?" Heather said with a grin.

"Well, your fearsome protector kindly left me some of my tendon, so I am grateful to him for that. He sure is protective of you."

"Oh, is he ever! He's only four pounds dripping wet, but inside that little body beats the heart of a lion!" Heather beamed with pride every time she talked about Ant.

For the five years they'd been together so far, he'd proved himself to be a fierce protector, indeed, and such a little love bug. Though he came from a reputable breeder who was also a prestigious judge for the Westminster Kennel Club shows, she had absolutely no desire to parade him around in front of others or breed him. The moment she met him, she felt a strong connection to him as he looked up with those warm brown eyes pleading for Heather to take him home with her. They'd been practically attached at the hip ever since then.

Before Heather knew it, Laura brought out their plates of delicious, aromatic stacks of pancakes. Both of her choices looked absolutely to die for, but growing up in New England, she just knew she had to try the Maine Event first. The lobster, enriched by the sweet butter on the pancakes, melted in her mouth practically on contact. Her taste buds stood on end, begging for more, more, more. "I've had so many different dishes with lobster in it, but this one certainly is in the running for my favorite. It's absolutely heavenly!" She grabbed one of the smaller pieces of lobster and handed it to Ant, who was already sitting pretty because of how incredible all the hot food smelled.

Lars laughed, then said, "By the way, I had the opportunity to see your namesake, Heather, growing wild in Scotland when I was in college and did a semester abroad."

"What a trip that must have been!" Heather grabbed a clean fork and dove right into the Hawaiian Hotcakes, and she was not disappointed with that choice either. Though it was a bit sweet, Heather had an undeniable sweet tooth that didn't stop at being a chocoholic. It was perfect for her, and she didn't ever want to stop eating it!

"It was! It comes in different shades, as you know, and it stretches for as far as the eye can see. I went with my friends backpacking across the U.K. and Scotland, and we even slept in a field for a night. We should have taken pictures, but back then, we weren't fixated on curating social media pages twenty-four hours a day and just enjoyed the experiences, rather than document them constantly."

After Heather took another memorable bite, she rejoined the conversation. "I know what you mean! I travel to exotic locales for my job to help source plants from around the world for our greenhouse, and I typically take only a few photos at each location. I prefer to immerse in the country's culture and especially the food scenes there without having the pressure of always uploading content all day."

A huge raindrop splattered down on each of their plates, which prompted Heather to gaze skyward. That cloud definitely appeared darker and larger than it was before. "You know what they say, Ant: April showers bring May flowers!" She laughed to herself, then turned to Lars. "Do you think we should try to finish some more or box it up for takeout now?"

"I think we have a bit more time, and it's so delightful out here with you and Ant, but I agree. That cloud looks like it means business. How is the food?"

"My tastebuds are having a field day! This has to be one of the most brilliant breakfasts I have ever had," Heather said as she managed to shove another bite into her mouth.

Both ate awhile longer as the drops grew larger and more frequent on their rapidly clearing plates.

"Speaking of flowers and plants, do you know what I really want to see?" Heather began, "The Bonsai Bonanza at Boston Botanical Gardens! I hear they sold out of the tickets months ago."

"You won't believe this, Heather, but I have two tickets for tonight plus a dinner reservation, which I have to cancel because Mom's arthritis is acting up, and this damp weather especially makes her joints ache. So, she's not up to the evening's adventures. Why don't you join me? You are so appreciative of the botany. My mom would feel glad the present didn't go to waste."

The raindrops suddenly increased in intensity as the cloud burst into a solid downpour.

"Ah! Our luck has run out. Grab Ant and your chocolate cosmo flowers from the bucket and head to the kitchen door. I'll take our plates and meet you there."

Heather scooped up her little dog and shielded him with her body as best she could. She hustled over to the back door of the kitchen where Laura waited with the door held wide open.

"I just was finishing up delivering plates to that table in the corner when I heard the thunder and came rushing over here to help you guys!"

Heather grinned at her as raindrops clung to her eyelids, and water dripped off her nose. Lars bustled in a second later with the dishes of half-eaten pancakes.

"I'm so glad you rescued the pancakes, Lars. They still look pretty good, but if you like, the kitchen can whip you guys up a fresh batch for takeout."

"No need. These are still perfectly fine, and I even rescued the muffin basket from the flood too!" Lars grinned as he pulled the basket out from under his arm. "That checkered cloth you lined it with proved a good covering against the rain."

"Now you are telling all our restaurant secrets! What am I going to do with you?" Everyone in the happy trio laughed.

"Here, let me box these up, and please go take that umbrella in the umbrella stand in the corner." Laura pointed to an overflowing umbrella stand next to the door. "Customers leave umbrellas all the time. You can borrow one for today and bring it back with you when you come next time. By the looks of it, I wouldn't doubt I'll be seeing you both again real soon," she said with a pointed look at how Lars had been drying Ant off with a small towel he had found lying around while Heather had appeared to lean into him while they spoke.

Heather smiled up at Lars. "Thank you for this delicious breakfast. What a lovely morning it has been, and the rain can't possibly diminish it for me."

"It has been lovely. Will you join me for dinner and the Bonsai Bonanza at the Gardens tonight?"

"I would so love your mother to experience all of that. She has such a thoughtful, kind son to give her such wonderful presents. But if you say she doesn't feel well, I'd love to go! How about I stop by to visit her in a few days and describe everything to her. Then she can feel a part of it all too." Heather was shocked to see a slight tear form in Lars' eyes, and she bet that the wetness wasn't from the raindrops.

He cleared his throat and began, "That is such a sweet thing to offer. My mom means everything to me and has supported me when I was young and didn't go into a traditional field in college. She was patient with my botanical interests and always sent me to summer camps filled with outdoor activities. I'd love for you to meet her, and if you could share your experiences with her, that would warm my heart to the fullest."

Heather lost track of time and space as she looked into

Lars' kind eyes. *Boy, have I missed having a deep connection with a man like this! He is everything I had always hoped for in a companion. How am I so lucky to have fallen into this sweet romance with the perfect guy?*

Laura gently cleared her throat as they both startled and pulled apart. "I hate to interrupt you two love birds here, but the thunder is getting louder, and in my opinion, you have a small opening right now if you leave before the deluge gets worse. You can finish up this tender conversation later. Here you go! Everything is boxed up, and I will reserve your favorite table, Lars, for next Sunday at 10 a.m. Something tells me you might just appear here with this lovely lady and her adorable dog." Laura gave them both a wink and gently patted Ant's head. "I have to go, but I'll have the muffin basket ready for you at 10 a.m., Heather!"

Heather felt a small blush creep across her cheeks as she realized she must have been mooning over Lars for a minute, then decided she didn't mind, not when she had this wonderful feeling inside from his warm attention.

Lars went to the door and opened the umbrella. He held it over them, and it seemed the right thing to do to lean into him to stay dry. They made their way back to her car, with him carrying the takeout boxes and her carrying Ant and the chocolate cosmos flowers. Once she safely deposited Ant back in the car and closed the door, she turned to him.

"What a wonderful morning this has been with you," Lars said.

She couldn't believe it. His head dipped down, and suddenly, there was the softest of kisses. Right when she was just starting to register all the endorphins flooding her body, he pulled back and grinned.

"That tasted like coconut syrup, maple syrup, and toasted almonds," he said with a laugh.

"Well, you did mention it's all mix and match and ala carte."

Ant started barking up a storm as he perceived the kiss as too much for him to bear. Both of them laughed at the sight of poor Ant jumping out of his skin and bounding around on the driver's seat as he pressed his nose against the window to register his protest of that intimacy.

"I think he doesn't totally trust you yet." Heather laughed.

"That will be taken care of quickly. I will make it my mission from here on out to recruit dear Ant to my side—just see if I don't!"

A huge clap of thunder startled them both, and Heather rushed to open her car door. "Scoot over, Anthurium, before we get struck by lightning!" Heather gently helped Ant go to his side on the passenger seat and turned to Lars once more. "Thank you for everything. The date tonight seems too good to be true, but I will feel less guilty now that we planned a visit with your mother to share my experiences."

"Absolutely! Drive safely. See you tonight! Bye, Ant!"

Hearing his name once more rekindled Ant's protective mechanism, and he started up again with a ferocious barking bout. Heather closed the door quickly before Lars got much wetter. With a friendly wave of her hand and one goodbye through a tiny beep of her horn, she pulled out into the early morning traffic and started her ride to William's Cot'.

"I hope you can start fresh with Lars, Ant, because I would like him in our lives." Heather's eye's opened wide when she realized what she just said, but she couldn't wipe the smile off her face. *Maybe he is the one I have been waiting for all along. He is starting to really grow on me.*

Feeling as giddy as she did when she went to her first prom in junior year of high school, she drove home slowly in the deluge. She dialed Holly from her Bluetooth in her car, but it went to Holly's voicemail.

"Holly, it's Heather. You won't believe this, but it seems I have a date tonight. Can you please help me with makeup? I haven't worn any in so long, and I was never good at applying it. See you at the Cot' soon!" Heather decided to stop in the drugstore on the way home to buy some makeup. This was the first date she'd had in years. Always prioritizing her career, it was time she also expanded her personal life. *And Lars will do. He'll do very nicely, thank you very much*, she thought, *very nicely indeed.*

NINE

When a drenched Heather and Ant walked through the front door of the Cot', William and Holly sat on the couch, quietly waiting for Heather to return from her grand adventure this morning. She looked back and forth between them—Holly had a look of remorse on her face, and William's face had judgment written all over it. They both looked expectantly at Heather, all except for Pansy. As usual, her gaze was focused on William as she sat there in his lap, waiting for him to pet her.

Heather didn't understand what could have happened over the few hours she had been gone, and at that point, she didn't care. She'd had such a lovely time with Lars that morning, and this evening had the makings to be even more spectacular.

"I'm so sorry, Heather! It slipped out. I swear . . . it was a complete accident." Holly stood up and walked into the kitchen, returning with a large pot of her home-brewed herbal tea. She poured Heather a generous helping and placed it on the table next to her.

"What's going on, guys? I don't understand." Heather

gulped down a large amount of the delicious, aromatic tea and placed it back down. "Does he know our secret?"

William stood up, Pansy still attached to his body, as usual. "Oh, he knows! He knows all about the *dead body* you've been being so secretive about. And he knows that you talked his girlfriend into breaking into a crime scene! What in the world were you two thinking?" He looked at Heather, then over at Holly, who still looked upset about the whole ordeal.

"Please don't be mad at Holly!" Heather begged. "Nothing like this has ever happened in my life, and I just didn't know what to do. I didn't want to go over there alone. I'm so sorry, William. Can you ever forgive me?"

William's face suddenly softened. "Wait a minute, Heather! I'm not mad at either of you. I'm more concerned than anything else. Holly is the love of my life, and you're one of my very best friends and mentors. I'd never forgive myself if something happened to either of you, and I did nothing to help."

"Oh," Heather said, feeling relieved that she hadn't destroyed one of her most treasured friendships. "You want to help? Is that what this is about?"

William walked over to Heather and hugged her tightly. "Yes, of course, I want to help you." He pulled away from the hug and smiled down at Heather. "Now, with all that business out of the way, is there anything I can do to help you through this traumatic situation?"

Holly stepped forward. "That's why I felt I had to tell him about it, Heather. So, please don't be mad. I think, more than anyone else, William has the chops to help us get closer to figuring out what happened at the potting shed.

Heather smiled at Holly. "No, of course, I'm not mad at you. But what are you thinking?"

"Another field trip to the potting shed, this time with Mr. Double Ph.D. Himself, William, the Walking Encyclopedia!"

William smiled sheepishly and admitted to Heather, "I do happen to like collecting doctorates in the botanical fields. It's a hobby."

"I've always known you to be one of the most exceptional scholars I have ever known, so I agree heartily with Holly! Let's show you the potting shed, and maybe you can find something to help figure out this mystery."

The three of them quickly donned black clothing from head to toe and jumped in her car. William had tried to dislodge himself from Pansy, but she fought back every time he tried to put her down. So, she became a little feline detective and accompanied them to the crime scene.

Soon enough, they arrived at her large estate. Like she had before, Heather pulled into the remote-controlled garage so nobody could tell from the outside they were there. Heather busted out the surgical gloves again before they all headed into the house.

"What? Do you have like a lifetime supply of these things?" Holly laughed as she put her gloves on and made jazz hands at William and Heather. "They make me feel like I'm on a diamond heist with a group of international jewel thieves!"

William shook his head at Holly as he put his gloves, snapping them tightly against his skin. "Lead the way, Professor Moore!"

When they stepped into the potting shed, William got right down to business and started looking around with his super-focused flower detective eyes. He looked over at Heather. "Where was the body found?" He followed the direction Heather pointed and looked inside the cabinet. It was empty. "Huh. Really? With how clean it is, you wouldn't even know anything had been in there."

"Yeah," Heather agreed, "except for the dead flowers."

"And don't forget the money we found." Holly pointed toward the cabinet.

"What are you talking about?" William asked. He dipped his head in farther but couldn't find anything at all in the cabinet. Pansy meowed in protest of all the movement. "Nope. There are no flowers in here—dead or otherwise." He slid his hand around in the cabinet. "I'm not feeling a treasure trove of money either."

Holly walked around the room, sniffing as she went. "Come to mention it, I don't smell the chocolate either."

Heather stopped and looked around the room. "That's weird. They were here the other day. What do you think happened?"

William held a stern look on his face. "Well, I guess it's a good thing I came with you two today. It's entirely possible the murderer showed up to get rid of some evidence. I would have lost my mind if someone ever did anything to hurt either of you!" He grabbed Holly in an embrace and kissed her face all over. "What kind of flowers were they?"

"Chocolate cosmos," both Holly and Heather said in unison.

"Hmm. The fact that they're gone tells me that they were involved in the murder somehow," William said as he continued to look around the room.

Heather shrugged. "Or maybe some critter got in here and took off with them."

"The money too?" Holly let out a stifled laugh. "I don't mean to laugh at such a serious situation, but I was just picturing a raccoon rolling in a bed of crisp twenty-dollar bills."

"You're right," Heather said. "It might seem random if it was only the flowers, but the money too? It's all definitely related to the murder."

William stepped outside the shed, and Heather and Holly followed him. He walked around the perimeter of the shed looking for any clues the police might have missed. "What do you think, Pansy? This crime scene almost looks too perfect, too clean. I don't trust it. There's got to be something here the murderer missed."

After he made a full circle around the shed, he got on his hands and knees to look underneath the shed. Pansy clung to him for dear life and he searched, sticking her claws in deeper. He wiped his hands over the dirt for several minutes until he popped back up with something brightly colored in his hands.

Heather stepped closer to William and inspected what he held in his hands. "What is that?"

William turned it over in his hands as he inspected it. Pansy batted at it with her paws. "It looks to be a piece of pottery . . . possibly . . . but I don't know. It looks too bright to be practical, though."

"What do you mean?" Holly asked. "I've seen plenty of bright pottery at the craft stores. Yellows and greens and pinks and purples—all kinds of colors."

"Oh, sure," William said, "but that kind of pottery is just to look at. It's not functional. Typically, pottery that bright has a certain amount of lead paint in it. Nothing would ever grow in a flower pot that was this bright. And correct me if I'm wrong, Heather, but didn't your grandfather make products specifically for florists and nurseries?"

"As far as I know, those are the only types of businesses he dealt with."

William shrugged. "It's kind of curious, then, isn't it?"

Holly walked over to inspect the piece of pottery William had found herself. "What do you think it means?"

"It could be a clue, or it could be just a distraction. I don't know. But if you want, I can take it to my lab on Monday and run some tests on it." William took off one of his gloves and wrapped the shard of pottery in it to protect it from getting contaminated. "Other than that, I think this scene is pretty clean. Maybe we should pack it up and head back to the Cot' before someone sees us hanging out at a crime scene."

HEATHER SAT IN FRONT OF HOLLY'S VANITY AS SHE CHECKED OUT her reflection in the mirror. She didn't hate the way she looked without makeup, but she wanted to make a good impression on Lars. It had been a long time since she'd gone on a date with a man, and she felt nervous enough about that. Maybe if she felt she looked flawless, that would save her from being so anxious about their first official date.

"Are you sure it's okay for me to leave Ant with you and William while I'm out with Lars tonight? I'm worried something bad might happen while I'm gone," Heather said.

"Oh, look at you!" Holly gushed while she pulled out an entire arsenal of makeup. "You sound like one of those helicopter moms dropping their kids off on their first day of preschool. Ant will be fine. Besides, he's having so much fun with Sweetpea that he probably won't even notice you're gone."

"Gee, thanks. You really know how to make a girl feel good!" Heather laughed, then turned around to face Holly. "But even more important than that, you've got to help me with my face. I don't even know where to begin with makeup. It's all so complicated now—contouring, highlighting, bronzer, concealer—"

Holly kneeled in front of Heather, grabbing her hands. "I'm going to stop you right there, young lady! You have natural beauty for days, so you don't need all that fancy scientific makeup mumbo jumbo. But if you're not that experienced, I can apply your makeup for tonight. Just sit back and let me do all the work. I don't want you to worry about a thing."

Before Holly could get started putting on Heather's makeup, they heard a commotion coming from the living room through the cracked bedroom door. She stood up to go shut the door, but it was too late. Pansy came darting into the bedroom, pushing Holly out of the way. Not far behind her was Sweetpea, followed by Sweetpea's new best friend, Ant. As Pansy ran circles around the bedroom, the dogs followed her, barking the entire way.

Pansy jumped onto the vanity and stopped to look at herself in the mirror, and she lingered a second too long. Sweetpea got ahold of her tail, pulling Pansy down as she tried to grab onto Heather's arms with her razor-sharp claws, drawing blood in a long line as Sweetpea continued to yank on her tail. Pansy hissed, growled, and meowed as she lost her hold on Heather and the vanity, falling on top of Sweetpea, who yelped as she ran into the living room.

In all the commotion, Holly's makeup case had gotten knocked over, and Ant sat in the middle of all her makeup, chewing his way through several containers of loose-powder eye shadow. With the colored powder now on the floor, Ant rolled around in it like a madman on a mission to beautify his entire body. By the time Heather could pull him away from the makeup, his entire face was covered in metallic blue eye shadow powder, and he smiled up at Heather as though he was saying, "Don't I look pretty?"

Heather tried to get mad at him, but she couldn't control her laughter as she got down on all fours with Holly to clean up the damage Ant had done. "I'm so sorry! He's normally so well-behaved."

Holly laughed. "Oh, Heather! You don't have to pretend with me. You seem to have forgotten that I was there to help you clean up the mess he made in your office on your first day back to Shellesby! But it's ok. We're no strangers to four-legged shenanigans."

William suddenly popped his head through the door. "Oh, goodness. I stepped outside for one minute, and the entire world falls apart!"

Heather ran out of the room to find Ant. When she finally caught up to him, all three of the animals had blue all over them as they cuddled up in the corner for a nap after wearing themselves out. William bounded after her, pulling her away from the animals.

"Don't worry about it. I'll give them all baths tonight, and they'll be as good as new by the time you return from your date," William said. "Really . . . it's okay."

Heather let out a deep sigh. "I'm starting to think this date is a really bad idea." On top of everything that had just happened with the circus of four-legged troublemakers, her mind was also plagued by what William had found at the potting shed. No matter which way her thoughts went, she was still left with the realization that maybe Sunny's disaster last year had something to do with why Mary had died. After all, if the pottery truly did have lead in the glaze, then Mary might have been implicated as responsible because she had a hand in designing and producing the orders the company received. But why in the world would that lead to her losing her life? Surely, there had to be some other explanation, and Heather would not rest until she figured out what that was.

Holly stepped out of the bedroom and tugged on Heather's arm. "Don't worry about all this. Come back to the bedroom, and I'll put your makeup on for real this time— even if I have to put a padlock on the door!"

About thirty minutes later, Holly turned Heather around to look in the mirror at her masterpiece. Heather couldn't believe what a difference a little bit of makeup made in both her appearance and her confidence.

"Holly, you are a legit artist! I think you could give Jackson Pollock a run for his money. I can't believe how beautiful I look."

"No, Ant is the Pollock! You, my dear, are the Mona Lisa."

With her makeup now perfected, Heather went over to her section of Holly's closet where she had kept all the clothes she had brought with her. But much to her dismay, she had only brought pajamas and work clothes with her. "Oh, no! I don't have anything cute to wear on my date. What do I do now?"

Holly rushed to her side, reassuring her, "Don't worry about that. I've got you covered—but not *too* covered." She pulled out a blue sequin dress that was cut low in the front and had a sexy slit up the side. "If this doesn't blow your date away, then there is something seriously wrong with him!" Holly left her alone with the dress so she could finish getting ready.

The mirror became a sea of sparkling blue water as Heather checked herself out in Holly's dress. Her eyes traveled down to show just how revealing the dress was, and she started having second thoughts about the date again. "How can I go out in public like this? Everyone's going to be staring at me."

Holly had snuck up on Heather and beamed at how amazing she looked in the dress. "That's kind of the point, you know."

Heather turned around to face Holly. "I can't wear this! This is too much."

"No, it's not. It's just enough. Your date is going to take one look at you, and his entire world is going to change. That's the power of great beauty, and you've got it in spades, my friend, both inside and out. Just take a deep breath and take a chance on yourself for once. You deserve this."

Deep down, Heather knew Holly was right. After all these years of living her life making single-serving dinners, she was finally due for a change. She let out a deep breath and stepped out of Holly's bedroom, ready to conquer the world —and Lars' heart—like a new woman.

TEN

"Heather, you look absolutely amazing. I love your dress—it just lights up your face so beautifully!" Lars held open the door to Earth, Water, and Sky, and Heather slipped through feeling on top of the world. Once inside, she had to suck in a breath at the opulence of the establishment. A small waterfall made up the wall behind the host desk, and there were large cages full of brightly colored parrots and cockatiels and some very beautiful finches. Huge potted palms lined the entranceway, and soft music played in the background. Her heels clicked on the polished floor as she took in the recessed lighting and comfortably dim surroundings. It was like taking a little vacation from the city of Boston to an opulent oasis of wealth, beauty, and glamour.

Paintings lined the walls, and wait staff whispered along silently in their dark, discreet uniforms as they carried one silver-covered serving dish after another from the kitchen area. The open kitchen dominated the far corner of the room, and a row of chefs could be seen sautéing, chopping, and molding ingredients onto China plates to be whisked out to the eager diners.

"Mr. Oslo, it's great to see you again, sir. We have your favorite table ready. Would you and your lovely dinner companion follow me, please?"

Lars held out his arm, and Heather slipped her hand through it. She was close enough to smell his aftershave and thought he looked very spiffy himself tonight. *What a day of culinary delights and a phenomenal dining companion,* she thought as she smiled at him.

They were led to a table not too close to the bustle of the open kitchen, over on the left side, that proved quieter than the tables they just passed. She slid onto the comfortable booth seat and gave her full attention to the server who appeared instantly at their table.

"Good evening, Mr. Oslo, how are you tonight, sir?" The server included her in his greeting smile.

"I'm doing well, Jared. Thank you for asking. It is my pleasure to introduce Ms. Moore to the culinary extravaganza you are presenting tonight. Both she and I cannot wait to be surprised by your delicacies."

"Indeed, Mr. Oslo and Ms. Moore," Jared said with a nod. "As you may have heard, we are a one-of-a-kind dining experience. Boston is in the heart of New England, and we want to showcase all the region has to offer. We uniquely do this from the bottom up, so to speak. Boston has some powerful currents that bring deep-sea delicacies to the shallower waters from time to time. So, our dinner will start with savory rarities from the depths of the sea. We will work our way up towards the surface of the water, with two more dishes sourced from those depths. Breaking the surface, now at sea level, we will treat you to three dishes sourced across New England at that altitude and then finish with three courses inspired by ingredients found in the mountain areas of our region, with our cloudberry souffle ending our culinary sampling of mouth-watering foods from the earth, water, and sky. So, without further ado, please let me take my leave and return with your first course. What can I bring you to drink, ma'am?"

Heather was still busily reviewing what he had just said but settled on fresh-brewed iced tea with mint, while Lars decided to start with a cappuccino.

As Jared left, Lars explained, "The menu here is devised daily by the chefs, based on availability. They have a sweet deal with some of those deep-sea tuna boats, who often get only one or two of those deep-sea fish Jared was talking about. They save those rare finds exclusively for this restaurant, so they really are the only ones in town doing this kind of thing. I warn you: the portions are very, very small, as like I said, they often only get one or two rare deep-sea fish per day or a handful of rare mushrooms from the deep woods. Some courses are naturally larger than others, but I have never left here hungry after all nine courses!"

Jared returned just then with the drinks, which he put carefully down on the table. "May I present your first course? Lanternfish, which usually live at a depth of 1,000 feet. They are so named for their ability to produce light from biolumi- nescence. Our tuna boat had a lucky day today and caught two lanternfish for our restaurant. That powerful storm we had the other day really churned up the seas, and here we are!" Jared delicately placed a China serving dish in front of Lars and Heather.

She looked down at the unique presentation. The center of the plate had a seaweed bunch as a serving dish, and inside the seaweed was a quarter-sized morsel of fish. The left side of the plate had a small lit votive candle, and the right side of the plate had a carved turnip. It was indeed the most unique plating Heather had ever seen.

Looking wordlessly at Lars, who was busily cutting the small portion of fish into tiny bites to lengthen the experience,

Heather also cut herself a bite, swished it around in the yellow mustard sauce that accompanied it, and closed her eyes while she chewed. It was the tastiest fish she had ever had, with a unique flavor that she couldn't even begin to describe. It tasted unlike tuna, yet more flavorful than salmon. The lit candle was a nod to the lighting effect these fish had. Bioluminescence allowed these fish to look lit up from the chemical reactions in their organs.

"How is it? Are you enjoying the lanternfish?" Lars asked after taking his first bite.

"This is so unbelievable. I am so sorry your mother's arthritis acted up because she is the one who should really be here enjoying this perfect meal. But I can tell you this is a treat beyond words to be able to experience this unique dining experience. I cannot express my gratitude enough."

"Why don't we think of it as celebrating your director-ship? That is a huge honor and big accomplishment and deserving of Earth, Water, and Sky." Lars raised his glass in a toast to Heather's new career at Shellesby, and she uttered a silent toast for her new romance with Lars.

Jared came back right then to simultaneously swipe the empty plates up and gently put the next course in front of them. "I'd like to present you with our second course. Jumbo prawns from the Maine coast. We are offering a delectable black pepper and sea salt butter for dipping. The sea salt is harvested from our private property off the Newport, Rhode Island, coast. Narraganset Bay has some salt flats that are known the world over. We are privileged to share this with you tonight. Please enjoy!"

"So, tell me something about you haven't shared with me yet," Lars said, putting down his fork to put all his focus on Heather. "We've got into some exciting . . . shall we say . . . situations . . . together, but we haven't had much time to get to know each other."

The thing that popped into Heather's mind immediately

was finding the dead body in her grandfather's potting shed, but that was certainly not first-date material. "Well, when I lived in Washington, D.C., before moving back here, I got to be known locally as the queen of D.C. tourism. When I first moved there, I made a goal with myself to go visit a new park, memorial, or tourist attraction every single day. My old blog is still online with pictures and stories about what happened at each tourist attraction. I think they still link it on the chamber's website, and there was a huge article in the *Washington Post* after I visited the last location on the 365th day."

"Wow! How fun! I'm going to have to check that out some time," Lars said.

"What about you? What kind of secrets are you hiding in that brain of yours?" Heather asked.

Lars took a bite of the jumbo prawns and prepared to answer Heather's question. "Well, here's something that might make you think I'm a little strange . . . but here goes! I was raised in a television-free household, and to this day, I have never owned a television—if you can believe it."

Heather was not a huge fan of the television herself, and she couldn't remember the last time she spent longer than an hour in front of her television. "Ah, that's not so strange. It's kind of smart. I only watch it myself on occasion when there's a sporting event I want to see or a news broadcast once in a while."

Jared arrived again, interrupting their focus on each other. "Our third course is a hefty tuna steak from our day boats. We are pairing this sushi-grade fish with algae and parsley sauce. Please do not prejudge when you hear the word algae. It has been described as tasting like watercress and is a most pleasant accompaniment for the wood plank grilled fish. A grilled whole spring onion tossed in a light pesto sauce finishes off this course. Enjoy!"

Heather looked down at the algae sauce, and her stomach

turned a bit as she considered how disgusting it might taste. She did love exotic cuisine, though, and she didn't want to reject it without trying it first. "Oh, look at me being all squeamish about the algae sauce! I don't know about that."

"What is the most exotic thing you've ever eaten?" Lars asked.

"I think in Asia, some of the ingredients they put on my plate were still alive, so I guess it would have to be that!" So, when she thought about it, trying this algae sauce probably wouldn't be the weirdest thing she'd ever tasted.

"Well, there you go! You are far ahead here already. That algae sauce isn't alive, and if I see it start to move, I'll rescue you and stab it to death with a fork!"

Oh, boy, Heather thought. *This is kryptonite, absolute kryptonite! Humor is my number-one favorite quality in a man, and Lars has it in spades.*

"To be honest, I felt as you did when I first tried it, but I must warn you—it is very tasty! I have even been known to beg Jared for a little side order of it so much did I enjoy the taste. And as you see, they only put the merest spoonful under the fish, in deference to squeamish diners such as yourself."

"Well, okay, I feel better that I am not the only coward to dine at Earth, Water, and Sky!" Heather exclaimed.

"I have another backup plan for you too." He reached into his pocket and drew out a small, wrapped piece of chocolate. "Sometimes Mom's allergies make food taste off, so I give her a little chocolate at the end of the meal to make her feel better. If your taste buds explode in a thousand pieces after the algae sauce, this chocolate will perform CPR and bring them back from the dead."

Wait a minute—he's funny, kind, and dispenses CHOCOLATE ON DEMAND? Can you say "man of your dreams," Heather? her heart demanded as it picked up its pace and burst with happiness and excitement. *I better get a grip here on my infatuation with him before I melt into a puddle on the floor!*

"That is so sweet of you, but I am going to screw up my courage and attempt the algae sauce without a safety net, so to speak. Here, I'm going in!" Heather bravely cut a piece of the succulent fish and boldly swirled it around in the algae sauce, purposely dipping it into a large amount to show her insecurities who was boss. She then closed her eyes as she popped it in her mouth and chewed slowly. A myriad of expressions crossed her face as she first registered how good it was. *Wow, this is incredible!* This joy was immediately replaced with a look of consternation as her eyes flew open, and she saw that she had scooped up all the sauce given to her in that one bite. One and done, but the problem was she didn't feel finished with the new sauce.

"Your expressions are priceless! I have already signaled Jared for a little extra sauce, as I knew you would love it once you got over your initial reluctance."

As if on cue, Jared came over with a small gravy boat full of algae sauce and a knowing smile.

"May I?" Lars indicated as he held the gravy boat over her fish. She almost gave herself whiplash as she nodded vigorously while she chewed.

"Please!" Heather decided this was one of the best fish dinners she had ever had and was just wiping her mouth on a napkin when Jared came over with the next dish.

"Our fourth course features baby new potatoes from Vermont. These are tossed in a house-made dill mayonnaise and paired with soft poached speckled hen's eggs. Please enjoy."

This was a very hearty portion, as compared to the tiny samples she had been served up until now. She was wondering if she would indeed leave the restaurant still hungry, as the previous portions were indeed notably small.

This was a healthy amount of delectable potato salad, and the speckled hen's eggs were poached to sheer perfection. "This is much bigger than all those other courses combined!"

"Yes, that is their *modus operandus*. They always serve at least one course that will make you quite full, and the rest are just exotic one-of-a-kind taste treats."

"Is there someone special you come here with besides your Mom?" *Oh please, let there be no one! I will be crushed if he has a girlfriend. I think I am falling for him but good!* Heather almost didn't think she could handle his answer to her question.

"Oh sure, I used to come all the time with Lillian. She was my sweetheart for five years. Her family comes from France, and her sister just had a baby, and she wanted to be close to her. She sent out hundreds of resumes and finally landed her dream job—assistant director of the Tuileries in downtown Paris!"

"Wow, what a plum assignment! The Tuileries gardens are world-famous because they were created by Catherine de Medici and are in the heart of the French capital. She must be living on cloud nine to be granted such a position." And speaking of cloud nine, Heather's mood had rapidly escalated into bliss as she heard that he didn't have a sweetheart anymore. Someone like him was so desirable she felt luckier and luckier every minute about that chance encounter with him in the Cambridge Flower Market.

"She is. So, we parted as the best of friends. I have moved on from her in the nicest possible way. There was no animosity; we loved each other. She just wants to relocate her life to living in Europe, and I want to live out my life here. How about you? Is there anyone special in your life?"

"No, I wish there was." She stopped for a moment, her face turning red as she thought she might like to get more serious with Lars. "Rising to the top of the horticultural world was all-consuming. I just came from a five-year stint as director of the National Botanical Gardens. So, being at the helm of Shellesby College is kind of a step down; however, I have just come into an inheritance of my grandfather's estate and decided to come live in the estate rather than sell it, so here I am!"

"And here we are!" Jared chimed in with perfect timing. "Your fifth course is a salad of spring greens, including sweet dandelion and baby romaine. These are paired with some wild mushrooms sourced in the Berkshires this morning. Included here are porcini mushrooms, chanterelles, and some morels. The wild mushrooms are tossed in a goat cheese dressing, and the plate is finished with some bacon-infused fresh focaccia breadcrumbs. Enjoy!"

"I don't know how much empty real estate I have available in my stomach!" Heather was very glad that Holly's borrowed dress she was wearing had extra room to breathe. She would have been positively miserable if it was any tighter.

"I know exactly what you mean! As I said, their portions are tiny until you get to that fourth course, where they give you the sizable portion. Don't worry; they are scaling back the portions again as the banquet moves along. They are experts at this thing and anticipate the diner's every need."

Right as Heather was about to take a bite of the mushrooms, her phone dinged from inside her purse. "I'm so sorry! I forgot to turn my phone on silent when we arrived." She had only planned to turn the volume of her phone down, but the text message she saw sent her into a panic: *I'm sorry to disturb you on your date, but something has happened with Ant. Please call as soon as you can!*

Without saying a word, Heather looked up at Lars with a look of sheer misery on her face, then ran to the bathroom to call Holly. She knew Holly wouldn't have sent that message if it wasn't serious. By the time she got into a private stall in the women's bathroom, all sorts of scenarios played in her mind, and they left her wondering if her baby boy was okay. She picked up the phone and dialed.

"He just has to be okay!" she exclaimed as she waited for Holly to answer.

ELEVEN

The phone was on its third ring, and Heather started to panic even more. Tears fell down her face as she waited impatiently for Holly to answer. "Come on, Holly! You can't leave me hanging!" She hung up right away and dialed Holly's number again, getting an answer on the first ring this time.

"I thought that would get you," Holly teased. "Don't worry! Everything's fine! I just wanted to get you away from your date to ask how everything is going."

Heather let out a deep sigh as her entire life flashed before her eyes. "That was absolutely mean! Don't you dare ever scare me like that again, Holly. Everything is fine. I need to get back out there. Goodness knows what he thought as I ran screaming from the table. But we are having a great time—I will say that much." After she hung up the phone, she checked her makeup before stepping back out into the restaurant and heading to the table.

Lars stood up and seemed to be as worried as Heather was when she ran to the bathroom. "Heather, you scared me! Is everything okay?"

"It's fine. I am sorry. My best friend played a dirty joke on me so she could get details about how the date was going." Heather shook her head and sat down at the table. "Now, where were we?"

Lars laughed and took his seat. "And how *is* the date going?"

Heather flashed a big smile at Lars and let out a flirtatious laugh. "It's going great. This has been an amazing night so far!"

"Well, hang on tight because it's about to get more amazing." Lars nodded toward Jared as he headed their way with the next course.

"Your sixth course is sourced from a lake high on up near Mt. Washington. We have gone through the deep-sea layers, and the sea-level layer, and now we are using ingredients found at higher altitudes. May I please present you with fresh wild salmon accompanied by fiddlehead ferns and early spring ramps? Enjoy!"

"Fiddlehead ferns are such a treat! I haven't had these in years," Heather said as she immediately sought out the tender green shoots with her fork like a heat-seeking missile. "They are so-named, because as they grow up from the forest floor, they initially are all coiled up like the scroll part of a fiddle, or violin, hence the name."

"Yes, a fitting name for such a delicious vegetable. These ramps are in the wild onion family, as you know, and I always love coming here in the spring for these seasonal delicacies."

"So, you said you moved into your grandfather's estate recently," Lars said, placing his fork down upon finishing the course. "Do you have any other family you're close to that lives nearby?"

"Well, there's my nephew, Oliver. We reconnected this past week when he came over to help me straighten up the house a bit. He's my brother's son," Heather said.

"And your brother?"

Heather placed her fork down and looked up at Lars.

"Unfortunately, my brother passed away a few years ago, so it's just Oliver and his mom. He's had a hard time adjusting to losing his father, so I'm trying to help him however I can."

Before Lars could offer his condolences, Jared showed up with even more food. "Your seventh course is a cheddar cheese sampler platter sourced from Vermont. You will enjoy mild, sharp, and smoked cheddar along with whole wheat toast points. A selection of our house-made pickles is also presented, including cornichons and rainbow beets. Enjoy!"

Heather picked up her white linen napkin and gently waved it around. "I must concede defeat! I am waving my white flag. This is too much food!"

Jared and Lars both laughed. "We at Earth, Water, and Sky seek to exceed diners' expectations, so we are thrilled that you are enjoying tonight's presentation, and we hope to see you again sometime."

"Oh, absolutely! That reminds me, Jared. Please tell the front desk to put us down for the table in six months. We can't wait!"

"Very good, sir, I will do that. Bon appétit!"

"Six months? I'm ready to come back here tomorrow. Just joking! I bet this meal costs more than the GDP of some industrialized nations!" So far today, Lars had treated her to two restaurants that had blown her away. With just one day holding so many delights, she couldn't even imagine what the future might hold should they continue to date each other.

Lars laughed. "Well, that is true. They say you get what you pay for, and considering we are getting delicacies from every corner of New England and the deep sea, their price is fairly modest, all told. But yes, you cannot come here more than twice a year—once every six months. They put this policy in effect because when they opened, they were sold out quickly with the first week's diners. They all rebooked multiple dinners to celebrate every holiday and birthday in their families, and the restaurant knew that new diners would never get a chance to experience it if they didn't step in with the six-month rule."

Now, it was time for dessert, as Jared headed toward the table with something quite spectacular. Lars noticed him coming and said, "Oh, Heather, please give Jared your full attention!"

Right then, Jared came bearing down on their table with a very dramatic display. He held silver serving dishes, and the chefs had placed some dry ice on the plates, and a type of fog was enveloping Jared and the plates as he walked.

"Is that dry ice? That is the solid form of carbon dioxide if I don't miss my guess!" Heather watched in awe as Jared walked back and forth in front of the fog.

"That is exactly right, Heather. You've seen that fog effect in theatrical productions, right? They use that in their fog machines in the wings of the stage. This is their second-to-last course. You might think nothing can beat this, but you would be wrong."

Jared stood next to the table to announce the next treat they'd be enjoying. "I would like to present you with your eighth course tonight. Fresh red currant pudding. These early red currants were sourced on the Vermont border near the Adirondacks. The pudding is paired with a chocolate sauce and freshly toasted marshmallows."

Heather couldn't believe the theatrics of the eighth course. After he gently put the plates with the dry ice down, she could feel the coolness of the fog as it poured over the sides of the plates in waves and made her forearms a little cold. As she watched the dry ice dissipate and the red currant pudding show itself, Jared took out a tiny caramelizer, which was a very small blowtorch that chefs used to caramelize the tops of crème brulée and other desserts. He applied the pen-sized blowtorch to the marshmallows on both of their plates, and she watched in real-time as the snowy whiteness of the spongy marshmallows turned a crispy golden brown as the tiny flame caramelized the sugars in the gooey marshmallow. When his task was finally complete and the dessert was presented fully, he made a little bow and silently stole away as Heather and Lars admired their dishes.

"How can they possibly top this, Lars?"

"Oh, I think they can, Heather," Lars mumbled gently around the pudding in his mouth. "These red currants can grow at high altitudes. I used to do nature summer camps in the Green Mountains of Vermont and spent many a pleasant afternoon picking them."

Heather wiped her mouth on the exquisite linen napkin. "I must thank you again for this outrageously wonderful meal and date. This isn't a dinner—this is an exotic vacation! I will cherish this night, and I can't wait to describe all these dishes to your mother."

"She will undoubtedly love to hear about this, as she is a rather picky eater, but these superb entrees always tempt her appetite to the fullest. We usually can't stop talking about our latest meal here for the next six months until our allotted reservation comes around again. Our next meal will be in the fall, which is a great time to come here. They do all sorts of things with mini-pumpkins. They carve a mini-pumpkin and pair it with a freshly baked tiny pumpkin pie and all sorts of other special treats. It's hard to know which season is the best. They pour their hearts into them all!"

Oh, goodness. He is thinking about a future for us. Planning for a six-month return trip to this restaurant is about as strong a commitment as a promise ring, her heart told her.

Still feeling a little nervous about leaving Ant behind, Heather kept checking her cell phone to make sure there wasn't an emergency with her best furry friend after all. Holly had scared her to death with her fake emergency, and she wasn't finished lecturing her about how she had upset her. Holly would certainly get an earful when Heather got back to the Cot', right after she told her about this incredible date, of course.

It didn't take long for them to destroy their portions of fresh red currant pudding, and it was right in time. Approaching their table from around the corner, Jared headed in their direction with a huge smile on his face. "Your ninth course is our cloudberry soufflé with blueberry sauce and fresh whipped cream. This is the culmination of your Earth, Water, and Sky experience tonight, and we leave you with a colorful sky image. Enjoy!"

Heather looked down and thought it was the prettiest plate she had ever seen. The entire plate was covered in a light glaze of blueberry sauce. She imagined this formed the sky of the image. The clouds were represented by carefully molded puffs of the fresh whipped cream, and the tiny cloudberry soufflé was gently centered in the midst of it all. The pastry chef had even carved a seagull out of a strawberry.

"This plate is as beautiful as an Impressionistic painting! I see what you mean by saving the best for last."

"Yes, indeed! I don't want to rush you, but I have just signaled Jared for the check because it is 9:30 p.m. already." Lars said.

"9:30 p.m.! I can't believe this! Did we lose track of time so badly?"

"I'm afraid so. It is a common occurrence for the first time here," Lars said with his trademark twinkle.

Heather started rapidly spooning in the soufflé and the fluffy clouds of whipped cream. "Okay, I'm finished," she mumbled with one hand in front of her mouth. "Rushing now because we can't miss the bonsai exhibit! If you're finished, too, let's try to make it."

"Absolutely," Lars agreed while he multitasked with one hand spooning in dessert, while the other hand signed the check. He slid out of the booth and held his hand out.

"Here, if you hold tight to me, maybe we can scoot along a bit faster. It is only a few blocks away, after all."

Heather tucked her arm tightly inside his, and they took off.

As they headed toward the entrance, the host called after Lars, "Goodbye, Mr. Oslo, we hope you enjoyed your meal tonight! We look forward to seeing you in the fall. Your reservation is confirmed!"

"Thank you so much, Charles. Perfection as usual!" Lars returned.

"Very grateful for the feedback, sir! And if you would please possibly consider writing us a review on Global Dining Fanatic's website, we are currently in the top spot for Best Restaurant in America. We could use every vote we can get, sir."

"*I* will write that review, Charles! I had the time of my life here, and I will make sure everyone knows about it!" Heather exclaimed as she waved her goodbyes.

Both men laughed at the vehemence in her voice, and with a final wave at the host, Lars navigated them out the door and down the sidewalk at top speed. With her heels on, she never could have walked this fast alone, but with him tightly holding her waist, she could speed-walk with him.

"This is reminding me of those three-legged races we did in the fall, with bobbing for apples and other innocent farm fun as a kid," Heather said as they sped toward their destination.

"Hah! I was just thinking the same thing myself, although I never had as sweet a partner to do it with as you. If memory serves, I was teamed with my cousin, who never had a great start, so we usually always ended up last in those races."

This is so much fun, Heather thought. *I could speed-walk the streets of Boston for hours with this amazing guy.*

Lars glided them quickly up the steps of the Boston Botanical Gardens and through the ornate doors where they came to a screeching halt. The Gardens occupied almost an acre of land in downtown Boston, a relic from an older era. It was started in 1779 and had survived many heated Boston City Council planning board meetings across the centuries. There just wasn't the will to demolish the Gardens in favor of more high-rises. The Gardens themselves were closed at night, but the organization held important lectures and kept displays in their main building open during certain evening hours. A security guard prevented them from entering any farther. "Excuse me, folks. You are quite late. The last timed tickets were for 8:30 p.m."

"Yes, yes, we are so sorry! Here they are." Lars produced them to show the guard.

"I am sorry, but we are closing in fifteen minutes. We can't afford overtime pay for the staff. We are asking everyone to leave the building now. No exceptions."

"Oh, no!" Heather said in dismay. "Is this the last day for the exhibit too?"

"Right you are, lady." The guard suddenly seemed to have a thought. "Well, seeing as it is the last day, and I know how rare this event is, I have an idea for you. If you come quickly and stay only five minutes, I can zip you in and out. My further suggestion is to take photos during your five minutes. That way you can spend time discussing the bonsai leisurely on your own later. Deal?"

"*Deal!*" Both Lars and Heather vigorously agreed.

"Follow me, folks."

The speed-walking continued now as Lars hustled them after the guard. Soon enough, they were ushered into the large display hall and beheld close to a hundred small bonsai plants growing in seemingly expensive decorative pots.

"Can you believe this is the first traveling exhibit from the emperor's household?"

"Are you getting good shots, Heather?" Lars inquired as he peered through the camera on his cellphone.

"Not only am I getting good shots—I already have them in the Valencia filter!"

"Folks, time waits for no one! You only have two more minutes here, so keep going with those photos! That way you can both become the rockstars of your social media platforms and dominate the newsfeed! Who can compete with pictures of royal bonsai plants? Unless, that is, that baby goat video is currently circulating. You might have a problem overtaking the baby goat. I've seen him—he's unbelievably cute!"

"I might just be able to take on the baby goat video with my secret weapon—the Valencia filter!" Heather laughed.

They both took enough photos to fill an entire external hard drive.

"Look at us! All our big talk at breakfast about not being held hostage to social media." Lars had to laugh.

"Usually, I don't take so many pictures, but royal bonsai are in a league of their own!"

"So true," Lars agreed.

Soon enough, they turned and followed the guard back out when he signaled it was time.

"Thank you so much! We appreciate the opportunity," Heather said as she was whisked toward the door as the large grandfather clock started booming at the top of the hour. She saw the large hand slide vertically into place as the chimes signaled 10:00 p.m. on the dot.

On the tenth chime, Lars waved over his shoulder a final farewell, then they slowed their pace as they walked down the stairs of the Gardens and back toward his car.

They drove home in a happy mood with both recalling their favorite dishes from their epic meal. As he held open the door for her when he pulled up at William's Cot', he leaned in for a kiss, and this time, she went up on her tiptoes and met him more than halfway. The butterflies in her tummy started up again, as she surmised they always would with this man who had captured her heart with his kindness, humor, and attractiveness.

After the kiss, he frowned in mock concentration. "Hmm, I wonder what *that* kiss tasted like?"

She peered into his eyes and saw the merry twinkle there, just as the penny dropped for her too.

"Like *algae sauce!*" They both said in unison.

"I will let you go and get a head start on uploading to social media to try to take on that baby goat! I will await your email when I get home."

"Absolutely! Lars, thank you for the best day in recent memory! I glow inside, and it's not coming from the lantern fish either!"

"I love your humor, Heather. It's one of many things that charm me." Lars grabbed her and went in for another kiss, lingering a bit longer this time. When he pulled away, their eyes latched onto each other, magnetized in place for one brief powerful moment.

Lars had simply taken her breath away with that last kiss, and her voice grew softer as she spoke to him. "I feel the exact same way. Your jokes make my day." Heather took one step backward toward the door, her eyes still locked on his. As he looked deep into her, time seemed to stop. If only she could grab it and make that moment last forever, maybe the rest of her life might fall into place. Maybe all the other chaos and uncertainty would be okay.

Their fingers finally separated, and Lars reluctantly walked to his car. Heather stood there watching him as he pulled out of the driveway and drove on down the street. As soon as he was out of sight, she took her high heels off and went skipping the rest of the way to the front door. Her happiness could not be contained!

TWELVE

Heather had stayed up a little too late with Holly Sunday night talking about how well her date had gone with Lars. And even when they had finished their conversation, Heather's mind was so busy reliving every single moment of her date that she simply couldn't shut it off. It had caused a permanent smile to be plastered across her face because she couldn't stop thinking about Lars and that last kiss he had planted on her lips.

Come Monday morning, both she and Holly were tired, but they still had to be professional and arrive to work on time—a fact William had reminded them of several times when he tried repeatedly to wake them.

Once they finally got to the campus, Heather realized Poppy was due to arrive any minute now. Their agreed-upon meeting time came and went, though, and with everything she knew about Poppy, it didn't exactly surprise her that she should be late this morning.

Heather impatiently tapped her foot as she consulted her watch for the fourth time in as many minutes. Poppy's lateness was messing with her schedule. She had invited Oliver to the West Shirestown Carnival that evening. The Carnival celebrated the town's incorporation in 1638. The rose-design promise ring that the police showed her was pressing on her mind, and she wanted to talk to Oliver about it, but first, she was going to revisit the vegetable gardens with Poppy.

As her patience was rapidly evaporating, Poppy sped into the parking lot of the greenhouse's Visitor Center and pulled up next to Heather with an abrupt stop.

"Hi, Heather! Sorry I am late."

Heather scooted around the golf cart and climbed into the passenger seat. "Ok, Poppy, no funny business today with detours or souped-up engines. Let's just take a nice leisurely ride to the vegetable gardens so I can talk with the program supervisor about the planting schedule."

They exited the parking lot and turned onto the dirt path that encircled the lake. As they rode along in silence, Heather could see Poppy surreptitiously checking her phone for incoming texts.

"You're quiet today. Anything wrong?" Heather asked, not sure she wanted to know the answer. Poppy was a loose cannon on the best of days, and after the last volatile golf cart ride with her, she was on her guard and wary.

"What did you say?" Poppy asked absentmindedly as she pocketed her cellphone for the time being.

"I asked you if there's anything wrong because you are so quiet." Heather assumed she was probably texting her boyfriend again, and that thought immediately set her on edge because it didn't work out too well the last time they had rode together.

"Well, there is something, but I don't want to talk about it."

"Okay." Heather felt she did her duty to be polite and was relieved herself that she didn't have to engage with Poppy further for the time being.

They rode along in silence for a few more minutes before Poppy suddenly turned off the dirt path, gunned the engine, and cut through the private property of the neighboring estate again.

"No, Poppy, no! I thought I made it clear that I didn't want to do this cut-through again." Heather hung on to the side of the golf cart as it started whizzing through the estate's southern border.

"I have to show you this. They have such a huge asparagus field. They couldn't possibly eat all that themselves. I think we should approach them for having our workers come and harvest the asparagus and donate them to the town's food bank. Look, it's over there!"

Heather followed Poppy's outstretched index finger and saw what looked like almost an acre of asparagus shooting up from the ground. She had never seen the vegetable grown before and marveled at the thousands of bright green hardy spears poking above the ground about seven full inches high.

Poppy brought the golf cart to a halt and turned to Heather. "Don't you think this is something we could harvest with our workers? I am sure the estate doesn't do much with it. Even if they ate asparagus for breakfast, lunch, and dinner, they'd take months to eat it all, and by then, it's spoiled."

"That doesn't mean we should feel entitled to their property just because we don't approve of what they do with it. What you're doing now is even more reckless than the last time! I want you to turn back right now! I don't feel safe with you—I don't feel safe at all." Heather started to feel a prickling on her skin like a sixth sense was being activated. She felt an ominous foreboding that she couldn't put her finger on. Before she had a chance to investigate her feelings further, the matter was taken out of her hands. She turned her head to the right and saw three gigantic Rottweilers sitting a foot away. A scream tore from her mouth, and that seemed to animate the guard dogs. They suddenly rushed forward and almost jumped into the golf cart.

"Ahhhhhhh! Poppy! Quick, get away from here!"

Poppy turned the engine back on at lightning speed as the snarling dogs descended on the cart. Barking up a storm and kicking into high gear, the little golf cart barely stayed out of reach of those powerful jaws.

"Someone must have informed on me! There was no way anyone could have seen us out there in that remote field. I would blame Mary, but she's dead!"

"What are you talking about, Poppy?" Heather's heart raced as fast as the formula one cars at the Indy 500 and now this disturbing piece of news. She vowed never to get in a golf cart with Poppy again.

Heather never heard dogs bark so loudly before. As they got closer to the golf cart, their barking started to hurt her ears, and she felt the beginning of a headache forming. Terror ripped through her to think of what might happen if those guard dogs got ahold of her.

"Here, check this out!" Poppy rummaged under her seat and threw a newspaper in Heather's lap before resuming her white-knuckle grip on the steering wheel and piloting them chaotically back to the opening in the chain-link fence.

Heather held the newspaper fast across her chest as she caught it while looking back at the seemingly ever-gaining snarling dog pack behind them in hot pursuit. The dogs howled and barked fiercely, and she could see a froth of saliva dripping out of their mouths. "I think they're foaming at the mouth, Poppy! If I die of rabies, I swear I will come back and haunt you something fierce."

Suddenly, Poppy swore in disbelief, and the golf cart made a 180-degree U-turn. Someone had boarded up the exit hole in the chain-link fence, and she had no choice but to return to the other door she had cut in the chain-link fence they had entered through merely minutes ago.

"This is crazy! No one knew I was coming through here. I always stayed hidden behind the pines, so this feels like someone was trying to get me in trouble. Did you read the front-page headline? They found Mary dead the other day, so as much as we mutually hated each other, it obviously wasn't her getting me in trouble this time."

"Wait a minute! Is she the student you were telling me about before?" Heather asked.

Poppy ignored her. As she careened the golf cart south and retraced the route they took so they could leave the estate grounds, Heather took a peek with one eye at the newspaper headline. It proclaimed that the body of Mary Rose had been found in a potting shed and that her parents had been notified. The other eye she kept trained behind her as the three Rottweilers were still in hot pursuit.

"Wow! I can't shake those dogs. We will be in trouble unless I do something. Oh, I know! I'll cut through their lily pond. I think it is only a few inches deep. We should be able to navigate it in the golf cart."

Rabid dogs, and now this? I am going to die today—I just know it! If not by a dog attack, then by drowning. Heather grabbed onto her seat with a firm grip. "Poppy! This is outrageous! I am going to see to it that you are removed from your job with the prison outreach program. You can't trespass on private property like this. And you didn't listen to me when I said to do no funny business on the ride today. You are irresponsible."

"I am trying my best, Heather! I just wanted to show you the asparagus fields." With that, Poppy noisily burst into tears and wiped her nose with the sleeve of her shirt.

"I am shaken up about Mary's death. I may have disliked her, but it says she likely died of blunt force trauma to the head, and I feel bad about trying to ruin her life as a sopho-more. She may have been a pain, but she didn't deserve to die!"

Heather wondered how much trouble she'd be in if she simply dived into the pond to get away from Poppy. But the dogs started barking again, reminding her of why that would be a huge mistake.

Poppy had now entered the lily pond at top speed and with a big fanfare of splashing. The water instantly entered the golf cart and soaked Heather's shoes and the bottom of her skirt. She quickly rescued her handbag from the floor of the golf cart and held it in her lap.

The maneuver into the lily pond had been a great escape tactic, though, as the three Rottweilers were stymied and had to resign themselves to barking in protest as they were left on the far shore of the lily pond.

"If I can just keep this going without the motor getting soaked, we may get out of here in one piece!" She stomped on the gas, and the little golf cart finally traversed the length of the shallow lily pond and zoomed out of it and toward the hole she had cut in the chain-link fence.

Both Heather and Poppy's eyes grew to the size of saucers when they saw the owner and two policemen standing in the doorway of the fence.

"Wow," Poppy said, defeated, as she slowed the golf cart to a crawl and made a full stop in front of the small assemblage.

"Hello, Ms. Moore," one of the police officers began. Heather recognized the officer from her visit to the police station the other day.

"Officers," Heather acknowledged them back.

"I want to press charges of trespassing against her," the estate owner began with narrowed eyes and an accusing look at Poppy. "I have had it with her entering my property uninvited every day. It is one thing for her to ride along the perimeter of my grounds but another thing entirely to access my vegetable fields!"

"Speaking of that, we have people who could help you harvest that asparagus and donate it to the food bank. You could do a lot for the community that way." Poppy refused to give up on her mission, even though she was in danger of going to jail again.

Heather was shocked to find out that the student Poppy had such a vendetta against was Mary Rose. This made her a clear front runner in her mental list of suspects she was currently considering. Poppy had mentioned the revenge she'd gotten on Mary. *But going from shoplifting to murder?* Heather shuddered to think Poppy was capable of that. After all, she seemed like she was trying to turn over a new leaf with this prison program she had set up for the other prisoners. *But is it too late for Poppy?*

"I'm just broken up about Mary's death! I wish I could go back and do everything differently with her." Poppy burst into tears again.

"Are you pressing charges?" The police asked the estate owner.

"Yes."

The police then moved to take Poppy into custody with her meltdown getting louder every second. "No! I was just trying to turn my life around too. I need this job! No one will employ me now."

"Tell it to the judge, lady." The officer read her rights and escorted her away. The three Rottweilers had made their way to the estate owner's side and sat quietly awaiting further instructions.

Heather had no choice but to gingerly lower herself into the driver's side of the golf cart and pressed an experimental foot against the gas pedal. The golf cart lurched forward, and she drove out of the hole Poppy had cut in the fence for the absolute last time. Gingerly driving around the dirt path until she was once again at the Visitor's Center parking lot, Heather's throbbing head was now turning into a pretty nasty migraine.

—◉—

THE TINNY CARNIVAL MUSIC IS NOT HELPING MY MIGRAINE ONE BIT, Heather thought.

She had driven back to William's Cot' to pack up her stuff so she could return to her estate. The incident this morning had taken years off Heather's life, and now she simply wanted life to return to normal, if such a thing was possible.

She was dreading taking her leave of William and Holly, and it did not disappoint. Pansy had to be practically surgically removed from Willam, and then she threw the biggest hissy fit Heather had ever seen.

Once she'd finally gotten her separated from William, she tore through the Cot' like a horror movie villain, grabbing onto the curtains and slicing them into shreds.

"I'm so sorry! I will replace your curtains, of course," Heather said as she managed to wrestle Pansy into her cat carrier.

As Pansy lay there comatose after her rage-fest, Holly had observed, "She's putting the 'cat' in catatonic," and Heather had to agree.

Now that the police had finished collecting all the evidence after one last trip to her home on Stonelily and released the autopsy findings and Mary's name in the paper, they had allowed her to return home. Once she arrived home, she took a hot shower to wash away the muddy water grime that had soaked her calves as they drove through the lily pond. Heather wished she could have had a nice cup of tea and relaxed with Ant for a while, or even taken a nap, but here she was, trying to figure out some more facts surrounding Mary's death and any possible involvement Oliver might have had. Meeting him on neutral ground, like at the carnival, seemed like a good way to try to get him to open up—if that annoying carnival music would just stop.

She texted Oliver again to see where he was, and he informed her, quite rudely, that she had said to meet her at 6:00 p.m., and it was now only five.

"No, I am sure I said five, Oliver, as I have work tomorrow, and I would like to get home eventually."

"Sorry, I'm not able to get there until six," he said before he abruptly hung up.

She realized with all the hullaballoo over Poppy's arrest and chaotic golf cart ride, that she hadn't taken time for lunch and decided to get some cotton candy to munch while she waited.

"Aunt Heather, Heather, her mind's as light as a feather," Oliver suddenly began, making Heather jump and shove the cotton candy stick into her face with fright. Thinking back to the time he jumped out at her in the library at her estate, she realized this was the second time he had sprang out of nowhere to scare her and she hoped it wasn't going to be a recurring thing. Feeling like her whole face was a sticky pink mass now, she deployed the one napkin she had. The dispenser had been almost empty at the cotton candy stand, and she used the lone napkin to wipe the goo off her face. She felt sweaty as well because the humidity was out of control due to the pending rain. She glanced skyward and judged that the rain bank was about an hour away and hoped to finish with Oliver and be back in her car before the deluge began.

"You gave me a fright and are rude besides . . . but anyway, what do you want to eat?" Heather asked her unkempt nephew.

"I always go for fried dough at the carnival," Oliver said as he headed to the stall.

While they stood in the long line waiting to order, Heather

leaned into Oliver and whispered, "I have to ask you, Oliver, why did you give Papa's ring to Mary?"

Oliver's eyes grew bigger, and he shook his head. "How did you know about that?" He took a step away from Heather. "Are you the reason why the cops questioned me about my involvement in Mary's death? I thought we were family. I thought—"

Heather went after Oliver to explain. "Oliver, there is a reason why the police asked me about the ring they found on Mary's body. I don't know how much they told you, but her body was found in Papa's potting shed after we had lunch." In Heather's mind, this had always made her question Oliver's involvement in Mary's death. He had an opportunity and a motive to kill her, but she still didn't want to believe he was capable of that unforgivable act.

"Did you tell them I killed Mary?" Oliver asked.

"No! I certainly did not. I don't think you killed Mary, but I was quite shocked to find out you had given her Nana's ring," Heather said.

"I guess I was stupid to think she would ever marry me. I mean, look at me . . . ever since Dad died, I've let my life just fall apart. She was the only light I had left. I promised her the world, and what good did it do me?" Oliver kept walking away from the food court and toward the rides.

"Where are you going? I thought we were going to eat first!" Heather said.

"I changed my mind. Let's go on the roller coaster. It'll be fun!" Oliver exclaimed.

"I hate roller coasters! Please, can't we do anything but that? They scare me to death!" Heather exclaimed.

Oliver grabbed Heather's hand and pulled her along toward the roller coaster. "You've got to get over your irrational fears, Aunt Heather. I promise . . . if you do this with me, we can talk more about Mary. Please?"

Heather reluctantly agreed to Oliver's request and

followed him to the line in front of the roller coaster. The entire time they stood there waiting for their turn, Heather still wasn't sure if she would go on. But once there was an entire line of people standing behind her, she couldn't change her mind now. After waiting for about fifteen minutes, it was finally their turn. Heather's hands shook as she stepped onto the roller coaster and sat down in her seat. She double-checked several times to make sure she had secured her seat belt perfectly.

The roller coaster jerked forward, and Heather screamed.

"Wow, Aunt Heather, what's wrong with you? We haven't even changed altitude!" Oliver laughed. "This is the safest place on earth. You should really stop being so uptight."

The ride went up and down, back and forth, and Heather wished she could be anywhere but there. She couldn't believe Oliver thought it was so funny to see her so frightened of the ride. *Is he trying to scare me on purpose?* It didn't make sense why he'd want to see Heather so distraught.

As soon as the ride pulled to a stop, Heather ran away from the ride with Oliver chasing after her. Unsure of what he had in store for her next, she turned to confront Oliver about the ride. "Do you enjoy seeing me so frightened? I was willing to go so you wouldn't have to do it alone, but it wasn't very nice of you to make fun of me for it."

"You need to lighten up, Aunt Heather. That was a fun ride, and you totally ruined it for me. I was just trying to make you laugh."

"Well, I didn't find it very funny!" Heather exclaimed.

Oliver tugged on her arm as he went to the back of the line for the rollercoaster again. "Let's go again! Maybe you'll have fun the second time around."

Heather pulled away from Oliver, determined to stay on solid ground. "No, thank you. I think I'll be going home now. I've had about all the fun I can handle."

Once Heather got to her car and sat safely behind the

wheel, she let out a deep sigh of relief. She couldn't wait to get back home and drink some tea to calm her nerves after that stressful rollercoaster ride. But, about a mile into her drive home, another danger presented itself. She looked in her rearview mirror to see a van following her much too closely as the driver flashed their headlights at her repeatedly. Heather was determined to ignore the careless driver and pressed on toward her destination.

Before long, the driver behind her started to escalate things a bit. They rear-ended Heather as she drove forward, honking their horn at her. Heather sped up to get away from the driver, and the driver behind her sped up to match her pace, then got out of the lane to drive next to her.

The honking continued, and Heather looked over to see what the problem was. She saw the "Thornton Flower Company" sign on the van, but she couldn't see the person driving. Heather turned her eyes back to the road, and the van veered into the side of her car, running her off the road.

As Heather's car pulled to a stop on the side of the road, the van sped away, leaving Heather shaking with fear as she wondered why someone at Sunny's flower shop would do such a thing. But the more she thought about it, the more scared she got, and she knew she'd never be able to drive the rest of the way home. Her thoughts immediately went to Lars.

Heather realized she always felt a deep sense of safety and security with him as if he would always help her. *I certainly hope he helps me now,* she thought as she rang his number and waited. Her heart beat faster every time the phone rang . . . until he answered. His voice calmed her immediately.

THIRTEEN

"Heather! What a pleasure it is to hear your voice. I have been watching the clock and waiting for your nightly email. It's almost seven. Have you decided to send me something earlier today?" Lars asked.

"Lars," Heather began, her voice a little shaky after the upset she just had. "Lars," Heather said again, "I need to ask you a favor. I can't talk about it right now, but something very upsetting happened, and I think it's best if I don't drive right now. Problem is, I am on the side of the road, and I need someone to drive my car and me home."

"Heather, what's wrong? You sound very shook up!"

"Oh, I am! I will share it all with you in the car. Can you please come to pick me up?"

"Absolutely. I'll ask a former student of mine to come with me. He now works on campus, too, and he will drive your car back to your house. You can come in my car. I'll drive the student home after I settle you."

"Oh, that is so kind of you, Lars. And I would never ask for something like this if it weren't dire." Heather's eyes teared up again, and she tried her hardest not to let on that she was crying. She didn't want Lars to see her as being weak.

"I know, Heather. You are one of the most independent women I know, so there must be something out of whack in your universe for you to feel this rattled. Let me go find my student. He is a graduate student who always is ready to pitch in to help with anything I need. We will be there as soon as possible."

"Thank you, Lars. I really appreciate it." Heather's mind raced, and she tried to put that disturbing scene into perspective.

Did someone at the flower shop try to kill me just now?

Everything was a complete blur to Heather as she saw Lars approach her vehicle several minutes later; he had wasted no time in coming to help her.

She opened the door as Lars got out of his car and walked over to hers. "Heather, what has happened? Are you injured?"

Heather shook her head. "No, thankfully not, but not for want of trying." She leaned up to whisper in his ear. "I think someone just tried to kill me. They ran me off the road. I am very shaken up."

"Heather! We need to go to the police!" Lars exclaimed.

"No, not right now. I want to go home and process this a bit. Please take me home, Lars."

"Okay, just come with me. You're safe now." He put his arms around her to calm her down a bit.

Heather heard the thunder and wished she could be home with her Ant, as she knew he would probably be scared, and he was used to her comforting him during storms.

When they reached his car, he turned to her. "Here you go. If you give me your keys, Keifer will drive your car home. He was one of my best and most trusted students, and he will take good care of your car."

"Thank you."

"Yes, ma'am. I will follow Professor Oslo's car home and meet you there." Keifer got into Heather's car as Heather gratefully slid into the passenger's seat of Lars' deluxe electric car. It had the most delicious pine scent she identified as his aftershave. She had been close enough to him a few times to smell it, and it was a thoroughly pleasant smell.

"Here, I have a blanket in the car because sometimes Mom's feet get cold with the air conditioning on. Perhaps you can dry your hair a bit with it."

With a grateful look, Heather accepted the blanket and squeezed some of the extra moisture out of her dripping locks.

"You must tell me what has happened." Lars expertly guided the car onto the road and gave a small beep as he saw Keifer pulled up ahead, waiting for him.

As Heather attempted to dry her hair, she let out a deep sigh of relief, realizing she was now safe and well on her way home. "Well, I don't know who was driving the van, but it was from a local florist shop. They started following me a little too closer, and I tried to speed up to get away, but they followed me. I'm not sure sure, but I think maybe they were trying to kill me!"

"I don't believe this! That is practically attempted murder. Heather! You can't stay at your house alone right now. They might come to your house. Can't we file a police report?"

Heather shook her head. She was concerned about Oliver's state of mind, but she wasn't sure if that was the right move. "Well, I want to think about this a little longer before I report it to the police." Lars didn't know about the murder investigation she was involved in, and she didn't think this was the right moment to spring it on him.

"By the way, where are we going? I'm leaving the town center now and just point me to your house."

"Please take Oakdale Road to the end and then turn left

on Stonelily. It's number three and on the left. Thank you," Heather said.

Soon enough, Lars had pulled into her vast driveway, and she saw in the side mirror that Keifer slid into the driveway behind them. Lars was out of the car in a flash holding her door open. "Let's get you inside right now."

Heather dug her key out of her bag and opened the door. Normally, she'd have heard Ant jumping around and barking up a storm to greet her, but as she suspected, he must have been spooked by the storm and was no place to be found. As she pushed open the large ornately carved wood door, she turned on the crystal chandeliers above so they flooded the entry hall with light.

"Heather, would you like me to stay the night with you while you process this terrible event?" Lars asked.

"Oh gosh, I didn't think about that, but it does sound very nice at the moment. What about Keifer?"

Keifer jumped in. "Mr. Oslo, do you want to stay here tonight? If you do, I can call my roommate and have him pick me up and take me home."

"Well, I can drop you home, Keifer, if you want. You've been very accommodating tonight. I can run you home and be back soon to help my friend, Professor Moore."

"No worries, Professor Oslo. I'll get my roommate to pick me up, and I can wait on her front porch and chat with my girlfriend. Professor Moore has those big rocking chairs out there, and I will be dry under the porch roof." Keifer stepped toward the door to head outside.

"You have been a very bright spot in all my classes throughout the years, and I'm so proud you are working beside me now at the college. I know that I speak for Professor Moore as well when I say that we are so appreciative of your help and flexibility tonight. I'll see you soon on campus."

"Sure thing. Take care and goodnight." Keifer let himself out the big front door.

Heather realized what had just happened—Lars Oslo, the man she thought she was falling for, was about to spend the night with her for the very first time. Her mind raced as she tried to figure out their sleeping arrangements. *Is he going to want to sleep with me? Oh, gosh! I haven't slept next to a man in years!*

"Well, this is a nice surprise and all, but I think I have an idea. I haven't yet packed up all of grandfather's belongings, so I think we might get you in some of his nightclothes for the evening. And then there is a shower for you while I put on the hot tea. I could use something to settle my stomach, and I want to also find my beloved Ant. He must be terrified by the thunder."

"Yes, I can even use his old bedroom if there is a bed in there," Lars offered.

"Oh yes, let's go upstairs." Heather led the way to her bedroom upstairs so she could find Ant and make sure he was okay. "Anthurium, my brave boy, where are you?" She could hear him whining under her bed and rushed to his side. Flinging herself on the floor, she held her arms open wide to encourage Ant to come out from his favorite hiding spot. "Have you been under there long? I'm sorry I was away so long, but I am here now."

Ant ran into her arms, and she scooped him up as she stood up.

He immediately began barking up a storm as he caught sight of Lars.

"Now, now, none of that. I am 'Team Heather' all the way, little guy, so no need to get yourself all worked up. Let me pet him awhile; I have a hypnotizing touch."

Heather angled Ant so he could gently pet him. As advertised, Lars smoothed his hand rhythmically down Ant's tiny back, and they could both see him visibly relaxing.

"Why don't you take a shower? I will take out Ant for a walk and start a little snack. You must be still shook up, and a hot shower will calm you. Don't worry about us. We will be fine!"

Heather saw that Ant had indeed settled down and decided a hot shower sounded good. She went into the bathroom as she saw Lars head downstairs with Ant and decided to run a quick bubble bath. Sliding under the bubbles, she felt like she took her first deep breath that day. Letting her mind process the day's upsetting events, she breathed in the lavender-scented bath oil she had generously poured into the water and decided to add some eucalyptus bath salts as well. The aromatic steam rising from the tub soothed her on a deep level, and she indulged in a fifteen-minute soak before reluctantly rising from the bathtub.

When she returned downstairs, Lars had Ant tucked under one arm as he gently stirred the eggs into an omelet with the other. He was softly crooning "Hound Dog" to Ant as he did so.

"Making an omelet, I see," Heather said, smiling.

Lars placed Ant down on the floor and approached Heather. "Omelet? This isn't just any omelet, my dear! It's the Lars special."

"The Lars special? What's in it?" Heather asked.

Lars slid the omelet onto a plate for Heather and placed it on the table. "It's a surprise, but I think you'll like it!"

When Heather bit into the omelet, it nearly melted in her mouth. With that incredible first bite, Lars' out-of-this-world cooking transported her to Greece. As she tasted the generous portion of feta cheese, she closed her eyes and let out a deep sigh. It left her speechless, hungry for more, and maybe a little more smitten with him all at the same time.

Next, it was Lars' turn to shower, so he went upstairs to do that, re-emerging into the kitchen twenty minutes later dressed in night clothes from the 1800s: a long buttoned-up dressing gown, long socks, and to complete the outfit, a nightcap with a long tassel.

Heather burst into laughter when he showed up. "Dressed to impress, I see!"

Lars spun around so Heather could get a good look at his snazzy outfit. "It makes my eyes pop, don't you think?"

Heather suddenly realized there was an elephant in the room, and it wasn't the ridiculous outfit Lars had put on. She frowned as she looked into his face, tears forming at the corner of her eyes. "Lars, I'm afraid I haven't been completely honest with you."

Lars went to her side and pulled her into a loving embrace. "What's going on? Tell me about it."

"It's going to sound pretty crazy," Heather said as she wiped tears from her eyes.

"Try me."

"Well, have you heard about the horticulture student at Shellesby who was found murdered in a potting shed this week?" Heather looked hopefully into his eyes, searching for an ounce of empathy. She was afraid he might go running away from her forever once she told him the truth, but she couldn't keep it from him any longer.

Lars nodded his head. "Of course, it's been all over the news."

"Well, that potting shed . . . *that* potting shed is in my back yard. I'm the one who found Mary Rose's dead body."

Lars stepped back, obviously in a bit of shock upon hearing that bombshell. "You what? You found a dead body on your property?"

"Yes, and I've been trying to figure out who killed her ever since. That's why I'm waiting to talk to the police about what happened. The owner of that shop was a suspect, and I have a feeling it's related to her murder. I just need to figure out how it's all connected before I call them."

Lars put his arm around her. "Heather, you must! You've

just had a dangerous encounter, and if the owner is the killer, your life could be in danger!" He cradled her face in his hands and bent down to kiss her passionately. "I care about you very much, and I don't know what I'd do if I ever found out he did something to harm you. Promise me you'll go to the police tomorrow."

Heather couldn't promise that.

"Heather?"

Heather backed away from him, her mind still in a chaotic mess after getting run off the road. "I'll think about it."

"Well, at least let me help you while you figure this out. Okay?"

Heather nodded her head slowly.

Lars let out a deep sigh and embraced her. "I suppose that will have to do for now." After he let go of Heather, he gave her a nervous smile. "Look, you've had a really long day. Why don't we go to sleep, then we can start fresh in the morning? Whatever help you need from me . . . whether it's your investigating sidekick . . . or your bodyguard . . . I'm here. Okay?"

Heather smiled and leaned into Lars, kissing his cheek. "I'd like that. And I am quite tired."

They both held hands as they walked upstairs. When they reached the top of the stairs, Heather went to her bedroom, and Lars went to his. She watched him walk away as she held Ant in her arms.

AFTER THEY BOTH ATE A HEALTHY BREAKFAST TOGETHER, Heather reminded herself of the promise Lars had given her the night before. As she put her dishes in the sink, she wondered if talking to the police was even necessary. If Lars could help her figure this out, maybe they could help put all the pieces of the investigative puzzle together.

"Were you serious about helping me?" Heather asked as she watched him play with Ant to occupy himself.

Lars looked up and smiled at Heather. "Of course! Where do we start?"

"Well, I was thinking we could go into my grandfather's library and do some snooping there. He still has quite a bit of old records from his business that could be helpful."

"Do you think that has something to do with Mary's murder?" Lars asked.

"Well, she did work for Papa, and her body was found out in the potting shed, which is where she did a lot of her work. So, I'm thinking it may be related to something that happened at work, at least. And it seems like the best place to start."

"Lead the way, my dear!" Lars exclaimed.

Heather sat down in her grandfather's oversized leather office chair and pulled open one of his drawers. The only thing she found inside was a key to the filing cabinet and an unopened letter to him without a return address.

Lars looked over her shoulder as she picked up. "Who do you think that's from?"

"I don't know, but it's worth a shot, don't you think?"

Heather opened the envelope carefully and read the letter out loud so Lars could hear:

I've tried to contact you multiple times to get this matter settled once and for all, but I've been unsuccessful so far. It's been several weeks since I've seen you, and in your absence, my entire life has been destroyed. My husband left me. My children won't talk to me. Several of my employees quit. And now, I'm mere pennies away from losing my business. You better watch your back because I'm coming for everything you have.

The letter was unsigned, and it looked like a woman's handwriting. But without knowing who sent it, Heather couldn't possibly know if it was related to Mary's murder or not. The only thing she knew that was true from the details in this letter, was at least it hadn't been sent by Oliver. And as soon as Heather thought about Oliver, she remembered something he had told her when he came to visit her last week.

"Wait a minute! Oliver told me he'd found a threatening letter, and I thought he was just joking at the time. If he was telling the truth, then there's definitely more to this story." Heather put the letter aside and turned to Lars. "We've got to keep searching!"

Heather grabbed the key and walked over to the filing cabinet, then unlocked it to see what other clues she could find. She pulled out a thick folder that was labeled with the previous year and brought it back over to the desk. Flipping through the contents, everything looked pretty normal—that was until she got to the last few pieces of paper in the folder.

She pulled out an invoice that was from October of the previous year, and in bright red type, she saw the words PRODUCT OUT OF STOCK. She looked across to see what he had ordered, and it looked to be a special paint they used to coat the pottery. "A-ha!" Heather exclaimed.

"A-ha? It just looks like a normal invoice," Lars said as he looked closer at the faded invoice.

"But what I haven't told you yet is what we found at the potting shed a couple of days ago." Heather kept searching and found another invoice dated that same month. "We found a shard of pottery underneath the shed."

"Well, that doesn't seem too far-fetched. How would that have anything to do with a sold-out pottery glaze?" Lars asked.

Heather pointed to the only item on the invoice she now held in her hand. "Well, Papa's regular glaze he used was out of stock, so he had to purchase some from a different company. This company right here." She shook the invoice in the air. "If you look closely, you can see that he only purchased a glaze from them."

"Yes, okay, sure. But I'm sure that happens regularly when you run a pottery company. Right?" Lars asked.

"Yes, but that shard we found . . ." Heather got excited because she felt like was getting closer to solving the mystery. "Lars, that shard we found? We *think* there might be lead in the glaze. And if there is . . . well, we just might be that much closer to figuring out why Mary was killed!"

"We are?" Lars still seemed a bit confused.

"Well, what if a certain florist had told you a story a few days ago about a bad batch of pots that nearly destroyed her business? A certain florist who had either ran you off the road or sent somebody to do it for her?" Heather jumped out of the chair with a renewed purpose and ran over to one of the bookcases in her grandfather's collection. She ran her fingers along the book spines until she found the one she was looking for: *Nature's Black Thumb: The Rise and Fall of the Lead-Based Paint Industry.* She pulled the book out and slapped it down on the desk.

As Heather flipped through the pages, a peculiar bookmark caught her eye. It was an old receipt, and some of the words had been rubbed off from the friction the book pages had generated. But Heather saw the invoice amount clearly: $67,000 for a crate of custom-designed pots. The companies name had been rubbed off the receipt, but Heather had a good idea of who that sale had been made to. As she skimmed over the text on those particular pages, she found a paragraph that had previously been highlighted:

Lead-based glaze or paint is much more dangerous to humans, but it can cause harm to plants and flowers. It is

*highly recommended to avoid the use of any lead-based
product during the manufacturing process of garden hoses,
gardening tools, watering cans, or pottery designed to house
plants or flowers. The lead can leach into the soil and slowly
kill anything growing inside, especially pottery.*

"Papa clearly was concerned about the pots from this receipt," Heather said as she held up the faded piece of paper. "And that florist told me she had tried to get a refund from him, and he refused." She stopped to think for a moment because that wasn't like him to ignore his duty to his customers. "But why? Papa's company received numerous awards for customer service. He most definitely would have refunded her money if she wasn't happy."

"Seems like maybe she decided to do something to exact her revenge for all that lost money," Lars said.

"She must have come to the estate looking for Papa, not knowing he had already died," Heather said.

"And, naturally, she would have needed to get vengeance on someone, right?" Lars asked.

"Right! So, she chose the next best thing—the artist who presumably put the lead-based glaze on the pot!" Heather exclaimed.

Heather jumped up and planted a kiss on Lars' lips, then set the book down on the table. "It's certainly not definitive; however, when you put all these things together—"

"Frankly, my dear, it sounds like we got ourselves a motive," Lars said, impersonating Rhett Butler from *Gone With the Wind.*

"Papa would never buy a glaze like that," Heather said. "He must not have known that it would have killed any flowers Sunny's customers tried to grow inside the pots." But there was still the issue with the refund. "I mean, it's a start, but I just have this gut feeling there's something more to this.

I would bet this entire estate on the fact that Papa would have refunded her that money for the damage it did to her business."

The front doorbell rang, interrupting their eureka moment. Heather realized she had yet to hear the doorbell since she moved into the estate. The chime was so loud it sounded like Big Ben in England.

The doorbell rang again, and they went to open it together.

Standing outside was a very contrite and unsure Oliver.

Ant immediately went into protective mode and remembered how Oliver had kicked him the last time they were together. He went for his Achilles heel, and failing to get a purchase on that, he contented himself with a large mouthful of Oliver's torn jeans. He shook his head back and forth as he snarled up a storm in his high-pitched voice.

"Are you here to make fun of me some more?" Heather asked. She let Ant have his revenge on Oliver and allowed him to keep munching on Oliver's pants.

"I'm sorry, Aunt Heather," Oliver began, trying not to get his tender skin caught in-between Ant's teeth. He tried gently to shake his leg free from the protective Chihuahua, but Ant proved committed to Oliver's leg.

"That's why I'm here. To apologize. What I did was immature, and I guess it was over the line. My only defense is that I was out of my right mind because my former fiancée had died, and I was lashing out from the stress of it all. Oh, ow!" Oliver grimaced as Ant found some of his tender calk skin.

With one leg being held fast by Ant, he awkwardly bent down and rummaged in a backpack he had taken off and placed near his feet. Straightening up, he showed Heather the front-page article about Mary's discovery.

"Ow, ow, ow," Oliver said quietly as Ant continued to shake his head back and forth with a mouthful of his pants.

"Aunt Heather! I always thought somewhere, somehow,

someway Mary and I would get back together. I let myself go after we broke up, but she was the best thing to happen to me, and I swear I would give anything to have her back. With Mary dead, I have nothing more to live for and hope for."

"Well, that's not true, Oliver. You have your whole life ahead of you, but this is a conversation that needs to happen over a longer period and not just in my doorway. Why don't you come over for dinner on Sunday? Come early, and we will talk. Maybe I can help you figure out what you'd like to do with the rest of your life."

Heather stepped forward and wrapped her arms around Oliver, squeezing him as tight as she might if her brother had been standing before her. Then she smiled even wider as she said, "I think your dad would be proud of you today. And that's certainly something!"

FOURTEEN

With all the local media now involved in the case of Mary Rose's homicide, the entire campus had started talking about her. News of her death had hit the local newspapers and television news, and social media. Even the national news took interest in the story because Shellesby College had risen in the ranks over the years as one of the top colleges for horticulture and botany. Heather had an important meeting on the books with President Johnson because she wanted to take action before their reputation as a prestigious school took a hit.

Heather felt as though everything was closing in on her tighter and tighter because as far as she knew, nobody knew Mary's body had been found at her residence—and she certainly wanted to keep it that way. *If I can prove who the murderer is—and soon—then this entire mess will go away. Nobody will even know that I or my family is involved in this horrible incident.* That was why meeting with William this morning was so important. If William was right about the lead-based glaze, then she'd be even closer to discovering the killer than she was yesterday.

When she arrived bright and early at William's lab, he was already inside, waiting for Heather so they could get started. "I've been here for a couple of hours already . . . couldn't sleep . . . and so, I've gotten everything ready for our tests this morning."

"Wow, you really are eager to help me with this! You don't know how much that means to me, William. You've been such great support through all of this." As Heather walked along the table, she saw he had prepared several solutions for testing the shard of pottery.

"See? What did I tell you? You should have come to me straight away. But no worries! We'll figure this out together." William pulled out a handful of microscope slides from a sterile container and pulled the piece of pottery out of its envelope. With a small tool, he carefully gathered some of the material from the piece of pottery and placed it on the slide. He pulled the microscope out and flipped on the projector so Heather could see the result displayed on the wall. William stepped back and explained what they were looking at.

As William pointed at an area of the slide that showed material angular in nature, he said, "We can clearly see that this area right here is the dirt from your back yard. They almost look like little sharp rocks in earthy colors." He pointed to another area that was deep red in color. "But this area over here is most definitely *not* dirt or soil. What does the color look like to you?"

Heather looked at the screen and saw specks of red with cracks running through it. "It looks like it could be—"

"Blood," William said. He looked over at Heather, and they both had a look of fright on their faces. "I think we'll set that aside for the authorities to look at."

"Wait a minute, William! I can't just go in there and tell them we broke into the crime scene. They'll think I'm the murderer they're looking for." Heather paced up and down the room as she imagined what would happen to her if they called the police.

"You don't have a choice. This is serious business, Heather! A girl has died, and we have a responsibility to tell the police what we know." William put the slide into a sterile container and turned back to Heather. "Before we do, I think we should test the shard to see if it has lead like I originally thought."

William pulled out two face masks and another set of gloves for Heather. "Here, put these on. I don't want you risking getting hurt if it does have lead in the paint." He sanitized a small tool so he could scrape some of the paint from the shard off carefully. Once he had a good sample of the glaze, he put it inside a glass vial, then poured a chemical solution into the vial. Once he had the cap securely on the vial, he shook the solution around to make sure it had a chance to penetrate the sample. "Ok, now, I've got to let it sit for a few minutes before the next step."

While they waited, William put what remained of the pottery fragment into a clear plastic bag, sealing it up so he could preserve it for the police. When the timer on his watch went off, he poured a few drops of a different solution into the vial, then shook it up again. "It shouldn't take long before we get a result from this chemical test. The liquid solution inside should turn a dark shade of yellow if it tests positive for lead."

As Heather watched the vial closely, she watched the chemical turn to a pale yellow, then it got gradually darker and darker until it stopped changing color. "Well, I guess that's it, huh? It's positive for lead?"

William nodded his head. "You got that right!"

"So, what does this mean?" Heather asked.

"Well, when you put the two clues together, it tells us that it's possible your victim was killed with a piece of pottery that was coated with a glaze that had lead paint in it. Beyond that, I think you should let the police take over as far as these clues are concerned."

Right as William was about to reach for his cell phone and hand it over to Heather to call the police, a knock came on the outside of the door to the lab. He carefully put away the specimens and opened the door to reveal a stressed-out Professor Dudley standing before him. William opened the door wider to show the professor that Heather was there with him too.

Dudley stepped into the lab, looking between William and Heather. The door slammed shut on its own, making everyone jump slightly. He slammed the morning newspaper down on the counter to reveal a huge headline that read: *SHELLESBY HORTICULTURE STUDENT FOUND DEAD AT PROFESSOR'S HOME.*

Heather's eyes practically bulged out of their sockets. She hadn't seen this new article yet, but now that she saw it with her own two eyes, all the talk around the college made sense. Her worst fears were now coming true—the world was that much closer to labeling her and her family as cold-blooded murderers. She grabbed the article in a panic and read through it while Dudley talked quietly to William. Nowhere in the article had they mentioned whose house Mary's body had been found at. While that made her feel a little bit better, it was still out there in the universe for all the amateur sleuths at Shellesby College to chip away at.

She threw the newspaper down on the table and pushed her way between Professor Dudley and William. "Why would they print such a thing?" She backed away from the newspaper until she ran into the wall. "They're practically saying—"

"I did it!" Professor Dudley yelled.

"What?" both William and Heather exclaimed at the same time.

"You . . . you killed Mary Rose?" Heather managed to get out, though she was still in shock.

"No . . . no . . . I misspoke. I mean, I *didn't* do it, if that's what you're wondering." He looked between Heather and William and wiped away the sweat pouring down his forehead.

William shot an admonishing look at Heather. "Why in the world would we think *you* killed Mary Rose?"

"Well, it's all right here, isn't it?" Dudley exclaimed, now pacing around the room. "Of course, they're keeping the name quiet, but the professor they're talking about is obvious, isn't it? I'm the only professor here who had a run-in with Mary."

Heather knew they hadn't found Mary's dead body at Dudley's home, but she ran the risk of exposure if she let on that she knew that. "Dudley, let's breathe here for just a minute." She stood in front of him and grabbed his hands. "Look at me and slow down for just a moment. Did they find Mary Rose's body at your home?"

"Well, no, but—"

Heather let go of Dudley's hands and offered an encouraging smile, even though she was filled with anxiety inside. "Okay, then. There's nothing else to do but let this pass, right?"

Professor Dudley offered a nervous smile. "Sure. Sure." Looking off in the distance, he looked as though he had something more to say.

"What is it, Dudley?" William asked. "What's wrong?"

As he paced around the room, Dudley explained, "Well, I didn't kill her, of course, but I think I know who did."

Both Heather and William had looks of shock on their faces. "You do?" they both asked in unison.

"Who do you think killed her?" Heather asked finally after a moment of awkward silence.

A campus police officer walked down the hallway and past William's laboratory. Though he had nothing to do with the murder investigation, it set Professor Dudley even further on edge, and he suddenly started shaking.

"I . . . I . . . I've got to go! I've already said too much!" Professor Dudley yelled, then darted out of the room.

Heather and William ran down the hallway after him and watched as he knocked several students over on his way out of the building. William looked over at Heather and pulled his cell phone out. "I'm calling the police right now. We've got to tell them about the blood, about Dudley, about everything. There is no time to waste!"

About thirty minutes after they called Detective Huff, he arrived at the campus with his forensics team because they had expected to collect some potential evidence for Mary Rose's homicide case. Upon their arrival, his lead forensic scientist, Dr. Spencer, put on a pair of surgical gloves so she could sample the shard of pottery they had found.

"I'm almost afraid to ask how you came in contact with this evidence," Detective Huff said, "and how long you've had it in your possession." He looked over Dr. Spencer's shoulder as she examined the evidence.

William and Heather exchanged a knowing look, but Heather knew she had to take a chance and tell the detective the truth. Her hands shook as she pushed her hair out of her face. "It was shortly . . . shortly before you finished investigating the crime scene." She waited for the detective to slap some handcuffs on her wrist. "I'm sorry . . . I . . . was just trying to clear my family's name." She looked down at the floor, afraid of what might happen next.

"I have a good mind to arrest both of you for tampering with evidence in a homicide case!" Detective Huff screamed. "Give me one good reason why I shouldn't!"

For the next several minutes, Heather explained everything they'd found on that last trip to the potting shed, then told him about all the details she uncovered with Lars the previous day. Then she went over to her briefcase to pull out the threatening letter, the two invoices, the receipt, and the book they'd found the receipt in. "You see, in a way, if we hadn't done all that—with all due respect, Detective . . . sir—we wouldn't be this close to helping you—"

Detective Huff interrupted her, "Helping? Is that what you think you're doing?" He let out a taunting laugh. "My dear, I'm afraid you're mistaken. What you've done is completely derailed our entire investigation!"

Dr. Spencer watched as Detective Huff grew angrier by the second. She cleared her throat first to get his attention, then when that didn't work, she raised her voice and said, "Detective! I've found something here!"

Everyone suddenly looked over at Dr. Spencer in surprise.

Dr. Spencer looked through the microscope again as William flipped a switch to show the slide on the projector screen. The doctor looked around the room, then got excited when she found a long pointer she could use, picking it up to illustrate what she had found. She tapped it on the projector screen that showed the same red spot William and Heather had studied earlier. "It might not be obvious to anyone else because your eyes aren't trained to notice these things, but if you look closely . . ."

Everyone crowded around the projector, squinting their eyes to see what the doctor was explaining.

". . . right on the edge of the crack of this dried blood is a circular ridge." She moved the pointer to indicate another. "And another right here, then another over here."

"What is it?" Detective Huff asked.

"What we've got is a partial fingerprint, and I think it's enough to run it through AFIS." She stood back and smiled at her discovery.

"AFIS? What's that?" Heather asked.

The look on Detective Huff's face softened, then got serious instead of angry. "It's the Automatic Fingerprint Identification System. And I'm willing to bet that if we get a match, it will lead us directly to our killer."

Everyone let out the breath they had been holding. Perhaps justice was coming for Mary Rose soon, and Heather couldn't wait.

FIFTEEN

When Heather arrived home from work that day, Detective Huff's anger lingered in her mind. As she went upstairs to change out of her work clothes, she wondered if she should just leave the investigation to the police. After all, they thought they had enough evidence to sniff out the killer once and for all. *Should I really concern myself with looking for more clues?* Even so, she didn't think there'd be anything left to search for in the shed. As Heather stepped into her overalls for the first time since she had found Mary's body, she suddenly remembered her grandfather's old garden was still a hot mess. *Maybe working on the garden will take my mind off the murder.*

Heather called Ant and Pansy as she ran downstairs to head outside to the garden. They followed her dutifully, ready for a nice day outside in the sun. Standing in front of the overgrown flower garden, Heather realized she had packed her gardening tools in a box that had inadvertently been stashed in the attic with her winter clothes, so she headed back toward the shed to grab some of her grandfather's old tools.

As she approached the shed, she heard a crash, and she

froze right where she stood. Heather felt in her pocket, but she didn't have her cell phone on her, so she couldn't call anybody for help. Though Ant was tiny, he was still her brave protector, so she spun around to look for him. Ant and Pansy were nowhere to be found. Her hands shook as she realized she was still in danger here by herself.

You're being ridiculous, Heather! It's probably just a raccoon looking for some food. It could have been true, but still, she felt paralyzed right where she stood in front of the shed.

Then she heard people talking. It sounded faint, but it was unmistakable—somebody was in her potting shed! When the voices got louder, she knew she was in trouble with no place nearby to hide. If she tried to run toward the house, she'd never have time to scoop up her beloved pets, and there was no way she could leave them behind. She would never forgive herself if something bad ever happened to them.

Heather saw the handle on the shed move. *This is it— you're about to come face to face with danger. Be brave. Be strong. Be fearless.*

The door swung open, and she locked eyes with someone familiar—Sunny Thornton.

And she wasn't alone.

Heather's esteemed colleague, Professor Dudley, stood right behind her.

Professor Dudley's words from earlier that day echoed in her mind: *I didn't kill her, but I think I know who did.*

"Sunny?" Heather was stunned. "Professor Dudley? What in the world are you doing here?" Then she looked at Sunny's hands and saw that she was holding the envelope of cash they'd found days ago when they were looking for clues. "What are you doing with that money? That doesn't belong to you!"

As the tension rose thick in the air, nobody spoke.

Heather's heart raced as she realized she was standing face-to-face with Mary Rose's killer. Dudley had been right with his admission. All the clues had been there staring Heather in the face . . .

. . . Sunny's failing business.

. . . the pottery disaster from last year.

. . . the chocolate cosmos she found in the shed.

. . . the blood-stained piece of pottery William had found.

. . . the lead in the paint.

. . . the dying flowers.

. . . the threatening letters.

Heather looked at Sunny as she gripped the tools Heather had found in the potting shed that traumatic day last week. Sunny's hands had practically turned completely white because of how hard she held onto those tools that had her company's name on them.

Heather stood tall as she confronted Sunny. "It was you! You killed—"

Professor Dudley backed away, moving into the darkness of the potting shed. Sunny looked back at him, then over at Heather. She was caught and had nowhere to escape to, just like Heather. She lunged at Heather, knocking her to the ground, dropping all the tools except for a pair of gold-plated pruning shears. Sunny dropped to the ground, jumping on top of Heather.

As Sunny held the shears to Heather's throat, she said, "What happens in the potting shed . . . stays in the potting shed."

"But why kill Mary? What did she have to do with any of this?" Heather asked as she struggled to get away. "Did you think she sabotaged your order on purpose?"

"Don't you see?" Sunny waved the pruning shears around. "This was about the money—this was always about the money. I came back to confront your grandfather, but he'd already died . . . I just didn't know it at the time. I turned to leave, and I saw *her* breaking into the shed. And that's when it all became clear."

"What happened?" Heather asked.

"*That girl* intercepted the refund that belonged to me. She stole *my* money and kept it for herself. She laughed in my face as she told me about her plan. I threatened to destroy her, threatened to make things worse for her if she didn't give me that money. She refused, and I lost it."

The money. That was why Mary had returned to the estate after Papa Moore had died. She must have gotten fired before she returned to retrieve the money, and Sunny had caught her right in the act!

Time seemed to stop for Heather as she felt the cold blade pressed up against her skin. Not even a second had passed before she felt the sharp blade against her neck, but it felt like an hour as everything around her moved in slow motion. She saw a butterfly in the distance on one lone flower that had held on fast and survived the dying garden. As it moved from petal to petal, she saw every millimeter of movement the butterfly made. But she saw something else in the corner of her eye that gave her hope—the butterfly's only nemesis that lived at the estate.

Ant thought he was going to destroy that butterfly—until he saw Heather in mortal danger. He stopped suddenly and turned his head, the fur on his back standing straight up. As Heather watched him leap toward her, he almost seemed like a superhero coming to save the day. He must have leaped several feet high, flying not so gracefully as his little legs swam through the air, finally landing right on Sunny.

Sunny screamed bloody murder and dropped the shears, rolling away from Heather's body long enough for Heather to grab onto the weapon Sunny had brandished. She pushed herself up and backed away from Sunny, pointing the weapon toward Sunny in case she got any bright ideas. As she focused on just trying to get them out of there alive, Ant lunged at Sunny as she lay on the ground screaming.

"Get him away from me! Help!" Sunny tried her hardest

to crawl away from Ant, but he stalked her everywhere she went, finally grabbing onto her jeans and shaking his head back and forth ferociously.

Professor Dudley stepped out of the shadows and into the doorway of the shed. "Heather, put the weapon down right now, or—"

"And why should I listen to you, Dudley? Huh? You were more than happy to sit idly by why Sunny murdered me! Is that what you did to Mary too?" As Heather screamed at Dudley, her tears streamed down her face and wouldn't stop. "You said before you thought you knew who killed her, which makes sense if you were there while it happened. Tell me the truth, Dudley. You didn't just think you knew who killed her, did you? You actually saw it with your own two eyes!"

"No, no. You've got me wrong! I didn't see her murder the poor girl, but I had my suspicions when she came home that night. She looked like she'd seen a ghost," Professor Dudley said.

"Is that why you ran from the police?" Heather asked.

Dudley's hands shook as he explained. "I guess I just panicked . . . thought they'd think I was involved. If it was actually true, you know . . . that . . . that—" He stopped talking suddenly and approached Heather. "I followed her here tonight to see what she was up to—I arrived right before you did."

"Don't . . . you . . . dare . . . say . . . a . . . word," Sunny managed to get out as she struggled with Ant. "I swear to God, if you say anything more, I will never speak to you again—and I'll take you for all your worth in divorce court!"

Heather looked from Sunny to Dudley, then back to Sunny again. "You're . . . you're . . . married to each other? That can't be!"

A sudden flash of anger appeared on Dudley's face as he turned to Sunny. "Divorce court? You've got to be kidding me! What good is that going to do when they send you to prison for killing Mary Rose?"

"You can't testify against me! We're still legally married!" Sunny screamed at Dudley.

Dudley laughed as he looked down at Sunny. "You're forgetting one thing, my little thorn. I have free will to testify against you if I want, and you can't do anything to stop me!"

His outburst had given Heather enough time to make it to the patio, only a few short feet away from the sliding glass door. Freedom was so close she could taste it, but she couldn't leave Ant and Pansy alone with these savages. As her heart threatened to burst right through her chest, she saw a little sign of safety from the corner of her eye. A police car rolled into her driveway, and two officers stepped out. One of those officers was out of uniform, and she recognized him. It was Detective Huff.

The detective came running toward the chain-link fence as soon as he saw the danger Heather was in, and he climbed over effortlessly, running toward Professor Dudley and Sunny. He pulled a convenient treat out of his pocket and gave it to Ant, who relinquished his hold on Sunny. As Detective Huff put handcuffs on her, Professor Dudley ran away from the scene, jumping over the fence and out of sight.

"Sunny Thornton, you're under arrest for the murder of Mary Rose. You have the right to remain silent . . ."

TWO HOURS LATER, HEATHER SAT SHIVERING AT THE POLICE station on a wooden bench next to Lars. He wrapped his blazer around her and held her closer to his body to warm her up. As he caressed her tussled-up hair, he leaned into her ear. "I'm here now. It's going to be okay."

Heather pulled away from him and looked into his eyes, noticing they showed signs of the tears he had cried when he received the call from Detective Huff telling him about what had happened to Heather. "You really do care about me, don't you?" She offered a weak smile as he kissed her forehead.

Lars let out a deep sigh and took Heather's face in his hands. "I'm afraid it's a bit more serious than that, Professor Moore. I think I'm falling in love with you."

Tears fell down Heather's face upon hearing those words, and she couldn't remember the last time she had cried tears of joy. Mary Rose's murderer had been arrested, and she had the blossoming love of an amazing man to look forward to.

SIXTEEN

Heather sat at her desk in the library in front of her laptop. She looked into the eyes of Melissa Rose, Mary's mother, on a video conference call and thought she saw a slight spark of hope in them. They had been on this phone call for an hour so far, and they'd shared many laughs, tears, and memories as they got to know each other. Melissa was in her mid-forties, but Heather could tell the death of her only child had aged her a bit in these past few weeks.

"Before we say our goodbyes, for now, I want to tell you how much I appreciate everything you're doing to create a legacy for Mary. It's such a shame that we had to meet under these circumstances, but from now on, you are an honorary member of the Rose Family. You are welcome to come to visit us in New York anytime you like," Melissa said.

"Thank you so much. That really means the world to me. And I'll keep you updated on the status of the Mary Rose scholarship we're setting up at Shellesby. It will take some time to put all the paperwork through, but once it gets going, I know her memory will make such a huge difference in our students' lives."

With that, the call disconnected, and Heather looked down at her watch. The last of the party guests would be showing up anytime now, and she wanted to make sure everything was set up and ready to go before everyone complained they were starving to death.

As she stepped out of the library, that seductive smell of chocolate assaulted her senses right away. Upon entering the kitchen, she saw Oliver and Lars working together to put frosting on the red velvet cupcakes that were bigger than Ant's head. Lars dipped a small spoon in the cream cheese frosting and offered Heather the first taste.

"Oh, my! You keep baking like that, and you won't ever be able to get rid of me," Heather said as she squeezed his hand.

Violet Oslo, Lars' mother, walked over from the kitchen sink. "And if he does, he's going to have to answer to me!"

Heather laughed and winked at Mrs. Oslo, then headed out to the living room where Holly and William were working together to set up the chocolate fountain. "Look, Heather!" Holly exclaimed. "I've set it up where one side is milk chocolate, the other side is dark chocolate, and I have some white chocolate chips on the top here if you're feeling a little frisky."

"Wow, Holly!" Heather exclaimed as her stomach begged her for a taste of five of everything she saw. "You've thought of everything."

As Heather reluctantly walked away from the chocolate fountain, the doorbell rang, and she ran to answer it. On the other side of the door was Keifer and his girlfriend, Julia, and they had brought some homemade chocolate-covered strawberries with them. As a thank-you for helping her after the fiasco with Oliver, Heather had asked Lars to invite them so she could properly show her gratitude.

"I'm so happy you could come, Keifer! And these look absolutely stunning. Lars is right there through the kitchen if you want to add them to the buffet of treats." Heather pointed the way to the kitchen as she looked around and felt a vague sense that something was missing. She just couldn't think of what it was.

Heather heard a bell ringing from a distance, and William started laughing behind her. "Oh, my Pansy is here! Don't you just love the new collar I bought her?"

"Love isn't the word I would use," Heather said with a laugh. That annoying bell had kept her up all night, tossing and turning while Pansy played with that disgusting stuffed mouse.

As soon as Pansy heard William's voice, the loudest meow Heather had ever heard rang out through the house, and she came bounding down the hallway. She jumped into William's outstretched arms. "There's my little girl! How's my Pansy-Wansy doing today? Aw. Did you miss me? Well, I missed you too! Can you kiss Daddy?"

"Yes, my love, get it out of your system while you can." Holly laughed and shook her head, then turned to Heather. "I swear, Pansy is all he's been talking about today! I have a mind to be a little jealous, but she's only a cat, after all! I don't think I need to worry."

Right then, William turned to her. "Only a cat?" He turned back to Pansy and covered her ears. "Don't you listen to Mommy! She doesn't know what she's saying."

The doorbell rang again, and Heather froze. She looked all around the room to see who all had arrived, and she didn't think they were missing anyone. "I wonder who that could be!" she said to herself. And when she opened the door, she got the shock of her life when she saw Poppy.

Poppy shoved a bunch of asparagus into Heather's hand. "I come bearing gifts!"

Heather stepped outside, then walked back in. "You haven't brought the golf cart with you, have you?" Heather laughed.

Poppy laughed. "No, just my bright, shiny self! And an apology." Poppy's voice softened as she looked up at Heather. "I swear, Professor Moore, I've learned my lesson. I am sorry about how everything went down at Shellesby. I've talked to my probation officer, and he's offered me another chance. I'm hoping you will too."

Heather sighed and brought in Poppy for a hug. "Oh, alright. We'll have a chat first thing Monday morning in my office, okay? And please don't be late this time, Poppy!"

"I promise to be on my best behavior."

Heather laughed as she started to walk away, then Poppy called after her.

"Professor Moore?"

Heather turned around. "Yes, Poppy?"

"One of the amends my probation officer asked me to make was with the property owner who pressed charges. We had a long chat, and he agreed to drop the charges if I promised to fix his fence."

"Oh, that's great, Poppy! It sounds like everything turned out amazing for you."

"I've just come from there, and there's something else too. He's agreed to sit down and have a meeting with us about a prison work-release program for the girls to help him out in his asparagus fields. So, I guess everything *did* turn out amazing, after all," Poppy said.

"Well, I think that's cause for celebration!" Heather exclaimed. "Why don't you join the party? It would be my pleasure to welcome you into my home today."

Poppy smiled and skipped into the kitchen to mingle with the other guests. Right as she did, William held a glass of champagne in the air and clanged his fork against it to get everybody's attention.

"Can everyone gather around? I have an important announcement to make!" William said.

"If this is about Pansy . . ." Holly mumbled under her breath.

Heather laughed and shook her head.

"I've just signed the contract with President Johnson this week! First thing Monday morning, plans for the Hudson Moore Memorial Library will be underway. We've secured a generous donation from an anonymous benefactor of five million dollars to start construction on a new library dedicated to Papa Moore, a true horticulture pioneer in our local community. Professor Moore has started off our 'budding' library by donating Hudson's entire collection of books," William said, urging everybody to raise their glasses in a toast. They all cheered to hear about the great news, and William waited for the room to quiet for his next announcement.

"And not only that, but we're in talks to create a ground-breaking lab on the top floor that will put my workspace to shame! President Johnson was so impressed by the proposal I put together that she promoted me to head of research and development at the Hudson Memorial Library."

"Here! Here!" Lars exclaimed, drinking down his glass of champagne. "I think this calls for a special treat! Who wants a chocolate martini?"

Heather's eyes practically bulged out of their sockets, and she raised her hand. "Oh! Pick me! Pick me!"

Lars walked over to Heather, leaning into her to whisper, "I already have, and it's the best decision I've made in my life so far."

Right as Heather leaned into Lars to return the sentiment, the doorbell rang again. Lars jumped up to beat Heather to do the door. "This is one of the many surprises I have arranged for the party!" He opened the door and welcomed a tall woman with long blond hair who held a small animal carrier. Lars welcomed her into Heather's home, and she set the carrier down on the floor. They hugged briefly, then he turned to the room.

"Hey, everyone! This is my sister, Iris Oslo," Lars announced, smiling.

Heather walked over to greet Iris. They exchanged smiles, laughter, and hugs as Lars introduced Heather as his girl-friend. "It's really nice to meet you," Heather said. "I've heard so many amazing things about you."

"Likewise!" Iris said, beaming back at Heather. "So, I've heard there's somebody in attendance with a bit of a cat prob-lem, and I've come bearing gifts as a solution." She bent down to the carrier and opened the door, pulling out an itty-bitty tortoiseshell kitten who had a smudge of orange on her forehead that looked like a flame. "This is Flare."

Holly rushed over to Iris and gushed over the cute little kitten. "Oh, my! Can I hold her? She's the cutest thing ever!" She whisked her away and sat down next to William on the couch, who was still attached at the hip to Pansy. Just awoken from a nap, the kitten opened her eyes and stared right at William. She put her paw out to touch him, purring with contentment. In response, Pansy hissed loudly, then jumped off William's lap, running down the hallway to sulk about the intruder.

"What is it with you and cats?" Holly shook her head as she handed the kitten over to him.

William shrugged. "Who knows? The universe is mysteri-ous. All I know is they are attracted to me like a moth to a flame—or should I say *flare*?" He laughed at his own joke, then turned to the kitten as she checked out his chest to make sure it made a suitable place for a nap.

Throughout the party, Oliver and Poppy had hidden out in the kitchen, so Heather went back to check on them. When she walked inside, they were standing together talking quietly, and Poppy was laughing at a secret joke Oliver had told.

"Seems like you two have made a new friend in each other," Heather said, interrupting their intimate moment.

"Yeah, Aunt Heather. It turns out we have a lot in common!" Oliver exclaimed.

"You mean, other than both having a police record!" Poppy joked as she play-hit his arm.

"She promised to give me a tour of Shellesby this week." Oliver offered a tentative smile to Heather. "I was thinking . . . I don't know . . . of maybe . . . maybe applying to attend there."

"Oliver, this is great news! As long as there are no golf carts involved, I approve!" Heather said, laughing. "I'll leave you two alone. Just wanted to make sure you were okay, Oliver."

Heather continued making her rounds around the room as the party raged on. By evening, people were starting to leave, and she wanted to check in with Holly and William before they took off for the night. "William, you better say your goodbyes to Pansy before you head out, or she will never forgive you."

William handed Flare over to Holly, then stood up, approaching Heather. "That reminds me!" He went to grab something he had set in the corner earlier. He unrolled the package to reveal a small Persian rug. "This is a Persian rug for my favorite *Purrsian* Pussycat! I wanted Pansy to have something warm and snuggly to curl up with in my absence."

Upon hearing her name called, Pansy came running into the room to check out the rug. Ant came running after her with Sweetpea, and they all did their duty sniffing out the rug to offer their canine approval. Pansy walked around and around to find her favorite spot, then curled up in a ball right in the middle of the rug. She batted her paws at the two dogs to chase them away. After all, this was *her* present from William, not theirs. No dogs allowed!

William laughed. "Well, it looks like I'm a hit with Pansy, yet again!"

Iris walked over to Holly and William as she was about to leave. "It seems like you two have fallen in love with Flare. Am I right?"

Holly and William looked up at each other with huge smiles on their faces. They both nodded enthusiastically at Iris, a little reluctant to hand Flare back to her. "I don't suppose she's up for adoption, is she?" Holly asked as she petted Flare.

"She is! And it looks like she's in good hands with you two," Iris said as she smiled.

"Really?" William's face lit up as he held onto Flare tightly. "We can keep her?"

"She's all yours! I know you'll give her a good home," Iris said.

Lars strolled up to the group, wrapping his arms around Iris. "Playing feline matchmaker again, are we?"

Iris laughed as she said, "Guilty as charged!" Then she turned to William and Holly. "I'll leave the carrier with you both—it has two of her favorite toys inside and a little bit of food to get you through the next couple of days."

With the party winding down now and most of the guests gone, Heather finally got a chance to relax with Lars and Violet on the couch with Ant cuddled up on Lars' lap and Pansy still napping on her substitute William. Heather sat next to Violet as she regaled her about the delightfully exotic dinner she had enjoyed with Lars on their first date.

"Oh, you *must* tell me about your experience with the algae and parsley sauce. That is a true rite of passage for anyone who attends one of the magnificent dinners at Earth, Water, and Sky." Violet smiled up at Heather, obviously excited to hear about what she had missed.

Heather remembered how truly unappetizing the sauce sounded when Jared and Lars had first told her about it. It was an adventure in fine dining if there ever was one! "Well, I have to admit that I was a little reluctant to try it at first. I simply closed my eyes and prayed for the best. It was like a wild rollercoaster ride in my mouth! It was truly surprising how delicious it was, and Lars had to flag down our server to get me some more sauce because I downed my portion all in one bite!"

Violet laughed and nodded her head. "My first experience with algae was much the same! But when you have a son as adventurous as mine, you have to throw some of your comforts out the window. He is always taking me to some-place new that I never really thought I would love. But he has a special sense for these things, doesn't he?"

Heather winked at Lars as she laughed. "Yes, he truly does! I am still dreaming of those pancakes from Pancake Paradise."

Lars laughed as he said, "By the way, we're due for another trip soon! You better get your taste buds ready."

"Oh, they were quite ready the moment I ate my last bite," Heather said.

When Violet turned to leave, she pulled Heather away from Lars for a private moment. After sharing a warm embrace, Violet said, "Heather, this has been such a great day! I can see now why Lars adores you so much. You let me know if he ever gets out of line, okay? After he told me about the incident at the Boston Flower Market, I was so mortified. He was taught much better manners than that!"

Heather laughed as she walked her to the door. "Oh, that's water under the bridge. Besides, it led to our first date, so he has been forgiven 100 times over." They hugged once more before she stepped outside.

Lars called out to her, "I'll be there in a moment, Mother! I just want to say goodbye to Heather before we take off."

The world seemed to stop as Lars looked deep into Heather's eyes. No words were said—they didn't need to.

The long, passionate kiss they shared was enough to carry Heather through to the next time she saw him. She knew there would be many more moments like this, and she looked forward to every single one of them.

Besides, she still had a little light left in the evening, and the garden wasn't going to plant itself.

If you enjoyed this story, please consider rating on Amazon!

WANT TO RECEIVE UPDATES FROM KRISTA ABOUT HER NEW BOOKS?

If you'd like to receive notifications when I send out free previews of my next books, you can sign up for my newsletter here:

https://kristalockheartauthor.com

ACKNOWLEDGMENTS

I would like to thank my creative team and Tina Morlock, specifically.

Tina is an extraordinary editor and a master in the literary world. I feel so grateful for Tina's creativity, imagination, and superior skill sets. My brainstorming sessions with Tina have been epic, and it brings me great joy to be able to share with you the fruits of those intensely creative sessions through this book. I found much of the book extremely funny and mostly typed the chapters through my tears of laughter on the computer.

I would also like to thank Daemon Manx for the continued sharpening.

ABOUT THE AUTHOR

Award-winning author Krista Lockheart writes irresistible cozy mysteries filled with humor and buzzworthy characters and plots. Her favorite activity is interacting with her readers from all over the world, and she enjoys their feedback and comments on her social media platforms. She loves good food, good conversation, and good books! Cooking is a passion, and she especially enjoys making pasta with vegetables. Chocolate, avocado, and seafood are her favorite foods to celebrate with.

Krista comes from an artistic background, and her art workshops sell out within a few hours of signup. Her work has earned cultural council grants and has been featured in newspapers, magazines, and on TV and on the radio.

In the past few months, her memoir and travel tales were published in the *Writer & Readers'* magazine, and her travel tale about her expedition to Peru was the editorial feature in *DRIFT Travel* magazine.

She contributed a short story to a Halloween anthology, and her debut novel was #1 in 12 categories on Amazon during its initial release (including in the Free Kindle Store and in New Release categories).

It also earned seven book awards, including winning the

Winter Pinnacle Book Achievement Awards in the romance category, First Place at *TheBookFest* in Humorous, a Second Place and Honorable Mention at *TheBookFest*, a First Place award from *Royal Dragonfly Book Awards*, being named a Finalist in the *Book Excellence Awards*, and a Silver Award from *Literary Titan*, along with five-star editorial reviews. Her book was recommended by *US Review of Books*, and the *Chick-Lit Cafe*, as well as featured in the *Midwest Book Review*.

Follow Krista Lockheart

https://www.facebook.com/Author-Krista-Lockheart-
https://www.instagram.com/authorkristalockheart
https://www.tiktok.com/@authorkristalockheart
https://www.amazon.com/Krista-Lockheart

ALSO BY KRISTA LOCKHEART

Did you enjoy *April Showers Bring Dead Flowers*? Check out
<u>BOOK 2</u>, now available for purchase on Amazon.

It's time to stop and smell the roses in this new book from critically acclaimed, award-winning, and bestselling cozy mystery author Krista Lockheart and Anna Little!

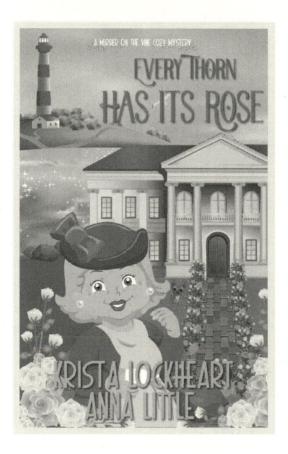

The Enchanted Twilight Rose is the only one of its kind, and people are literally dying to get their hands on it in this charming, witty, fun, and addictive cozy mystery.

Set in an elegant millionaire's mansion in the spectacular seaside setting of Newport, Rhode Island, greenhouse expert and botany Professor Heather Moore returns in **Book 2 of the *Murder on the Vine Cozy Mystery* series.** This time, she's excited about a new adventure when she goes to stay at the Ellis Estate at the request of the President of Shellesby College.

However, she doesn't quite expect all the twists and turns that she and her charming Chihuahua, Ant, experience at the sprawling estate that's the proud home of the world-renowned Enchanted Twilight Rose.

There, she meets Lauren, the woman of the house who swears up and down she's being haunted by a ghost. The estate cook, Victor, will do anything to get his hands on those priceless roses. But Amalia, who owns a local bath and body shop, is obsessed with the roses, too—and she is not Lauren's biggest fan . . . not by a long shot.

But this is nothing compared to suddenly finding an estate employee dead while Heather is busy solving the mystery of the ghost!

The Enchanted Twilight Rose is worth hundreds of thousands of dollars, and everyone at the Ellis estate will stop at nothing to get at them . . . that is, if they don't get caught on the thorns!

Every Thorn Has Its Rose is the second novel in the *Murder on the Vine Cozy Mystery* series. Join Heather and Ant as they explore the seedy underworld of gardens, greenhouses, and six-figure roses in this 'unputdownable' murder mystery mixed in with just a dash of romance!

Readers adore the *Murder on the Vine* cozy mysteries:

". . . had me totally hooked . . ."

". . . laugh out loud adorable . . ."

". . . just so funny . . ."

" . . . exceptionally great cozy mystery . . ."

". . . lovely jaunt into the botanical world . . ."

"... one you certainly shouldn't miss ..."

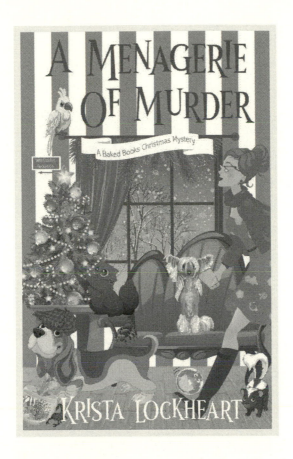

Introducing Adelaide Pascal and Truman Capote Pascal, a bookshop owner and Basset Hound sleuth team. This fun, new, exciting series—*Baked Books Mysteries*—debuted as an AMAZON BESTSELLER in September 2022.

All aboard the Christmas train to a cute and charming cozy mystery with a menagerie of animals that will make you smile! If you love animals, this short story is for YOU!

With a main character who is smart and creative and a heartwarming holiday setting, this fast-paced whodunit will brighten your day like it's Christmas morning! Enjoy holiday mirth with a cozy mystery flair.

Squeezing into the very last parking spot at Dr. Barker's veterinarian clinic, Adelaide Pascal and her charming Basset Hound, Truman, burst into the overflowing waiting room **to find more chaos than you can shake a snow globe at.** With the staff out sick, it's just the doctor on duty today and a menagerie of patients to see. **Everything is all jingle bells and hot chocolate** until Adelaide finds the doctor dead in his office. A blinding snowstorm means no one has come in or out for the last hour.

With her brave hound dog, Truman, Adelaide sets out to solve the murder mystery. Who could possibly have a motive to kill the vet?

Could it be the man with the poisonous lionfish? How about the teenager with the scorpion? The Persian cat owner who claims the vet won't provide a life-saving surgery for her beloved pet? The owner of the Chinese Crested dog who has a chip on his shoulder a mile high, claiming the vet botched a surgery on his Mom's beloved cat?

With a waiting room teeming with a baby skunk, three dogs, a cat, a tarantula, a scorpion, a cockatiel, a lionfish, and a hamster, **EVERYONE IS A SUSPECT** until Adelaide uncovers a hidden clue that leads directly to the killer.

This super charming cozy mystery short story will go down as easily as Christmas cookies & chilled milk. Join Adelaide and Truman in this cute tale for a fun read!

<u>Readers adore the *Baked Book Mysteries*</u>:

"... Truman's level of adorableness can't be denied ..."

"... gets you in the holiday mood ..."

"... delightful cozy mystery that will have you smiling ..."

"... a real winner of a tale ..."

"... had me cracking up ..."

"... a charming quick read ..."

Made in the USA
Middletown, DE
06 December 2022

17259168R00128